AF541667

The Hidden Letters...

The Hidden Letters...

Purba Chakraborty

BLUEJAY

Bluejay Books Pvt. Ltd.
A-8/76, Ist Floor
Sector 16, Rohini
Delhi 110 085
info@bluejaybooksindia.com

First published in 2014 by
Bluejay Books Pvt. Ltd.

Copyright © Purba Chakraborty, 2014

The author asserts the moral right to be identified as the author of this work.

All rights reserved. No part of this publication may be reproduced, stored in a retrieval system, or transmitted, in any form or by any means, electronic, mechanical, photocopying, recording or otherwise, without the prior written permission of the Publishers.

Typeset by Eshu Graphic

Printed and bound in India

To my parents' unconditional love for each other.

Acknowledgements

There is no better joy for me than writing a book. Writing is like food to my soul and I thank God for bestowing me with a creative mind. I thank Mom for all her blessings and always being with me in spirit. I hope wherever she is today, she is happy to see me as a writer.

Every time I started writing a book, I was completely lost in my characters and turned a little moody. It was not easy, writing this book without getting into the skin of the characters, which often left me emotionally exhausted. I must thank my father and my grandmother for bearing with my mood swings and for listening to me patiently, whenever I started talking about my protagonist and her dilemmas and miseries. You two are the best!

Thanks to my best friend, Priyam for making time to read every chapter of this book once I finished writing it down. Even if it had been 3 a.m., she would still insist that I send her the chapter and then we would talk about it in the wee hours of morning. You are my favourite reader, babes. Love you!

I also wish to mention the role of my closest friend Sisir, who was extremely encouraging and supportive right from the time I tried my hands at writing. I was passing through a really rough time in my life when I was writing this book, but his presence and words made me believe in myself. Lots of love and thanks!

A big thank you to my friends Priyanka, Samraggi, Ranamita and Sagar for reading the synopsis and giving me their valuable feedback.

Thanks to all my other friends for constantly asking me how my new book was progressing and for supporting me throughout.

Heartfelt thanks to all the readers of my first book, who kept asking me when my next book would be out and telling me that they couldn't wait to read it. You people are like my extended family. I value each one of you and I hope you love reading this book too.

And also a big thank you to the Bluejay team.

With some beautiful lines of my favourite poem by Rabindranath Tagore, I welcome you all to *The Hidden Letters...*

If thou speakest not, I will fill my heart with thy silence and endure it.

I will keep still and wait like the night,

With starry vigil and its head bent low with patience.

The morning will surely come,

The darkness will vanish,

And thy voices pour down in golden streams breaking through the sky.

Then thy words will take wing in songs

From every one of my birds' nests,

And thy melodies will break forth in flowers

In all my forest groves.

Prologue

James Joyce has rightly said, "Men are governed by lines of intellect - women: by curves of emotion." Practically, this is the only reason men find women complicated, capricious and episodic. A woman desires to be a man's last romance, her baby's first love and a person who can live with dignity all her life. As a girl matures to be a woman, her fairy tale imagination gets superseded by her struggle to be a good wife, a good mother and most importantly, a woman of virtue. As victor or vanquished, a woman keeps fighting the sequence of odds and evens throughout her life. Since nature has made women strong, society has very wisely done the reverse to maintain the balance. This is the story of one such woman who endeavoured to gain her husband's love, her daughter's respect and live a life of dignity by following her dreams. It is not really feasible to understand a woman when she is living three roles at the same time...a wife, a mother and a woman. The tremendous catastrophe that hits her life compels her to stand by one character out of the three. Either she has to vanquish the woman in her to make the wife win, or has to defeat the mother in her. Tough indeed...isn't it?

THE INDETERMINATE WRITER

Olivia looked at her mother with a sense of utmost pride as the latter's name was announced as the winner of "The indeterminate writer of the decade". Anaya Chatterjee hugged her daughter endearingly and approached the stage with vanity wrapped under her dignified stature. The audience with hundreds of people clapped as her name was announced, while the education minister and the founder of this literary prize – Mr. Umashankar Nath – waited for her to receive the prize. Anaya Chatterjee, winner of many national and international literary prizes, the writer of six international bestsellers, received the golden award. She was a woman in her mid-forties and stood a towering five feet seven; her beautiful face was enough to deceive people about her age. Dressed in a chocolate brown suit which enhanced her milk-white complexion, she could even give her eighteen-year-old daughter Olivia tough competition. She let her deep brown hair loose, cascading to her waist, and looked at the crowd with her dark charcoal eyes with a sense of victory as her pink lips curved into a half-smile. She received this prestigious award during the Kolkata Book Fair, in front of her daughter and in-laws, though her husband was missing. She missed Nishith and imagined him to be present among the cheerful crowd, clapping with utmost enthusiasm, waiting for her to speak.

"Thank you Mr. Nath, thank you Kolkata and thank you all my readers for giving me this." She started speaking as the crowd cheered for her.

"Fifteen years back, I was an ordinary woman. I never knew I had a writer within me. But when I started writing, I felt writing was my soul's medicine. I had to write to survive. As you all know, all my books are largely based on love, feminism and spirituality. My latest book, *The Obsession to Self-realization* deals with a woman who tries to realize herself, her own desires and wishes when her husband leaves her for another woman, hurting her self-respect.

"Writing is a sort of meditation for me; when I write, I can sense the purity in my soul which I can otherwise never feel. I owe a lot to my readers who have supported me right from the beginning when I was a newbie, especially my Kolkata readers. I also owe a lot to my loving family, my dear husband who is right now performing a surgery. His guidance, love and wishes are always around me like a veil. My daughter Olivia, who thinks her mom is the most beautiful and intelligent woman on this planet. Thanks my baby! My in-laws, Ma, Baba, you have never let me feel like an orphan and have always been my greatest fans. I have been lucky and blessed by the Almighty to have such a wonderful family. Thank you all."

"Mom, you are the best! I love you," Olivia came running to the teary-eyed Anaya as she came down from the stage.

"Love you Oli. Let's call your dad."Olivia dialled her dad's number and started telling him everything about the book fair and the award ceremony.

"Oli, give me the phone," Anaya patted her. "Hey…missed you a lot! I always wanted you to be there when I win an award at your native place… Yes, I know for you, your patients are more important than your wife… By the way, mister, I also have tons of fans, some of them are more interesting than you… Do you mean that Nishith?... No, I have seen your colleagues, they are boring… Stop making me jealous… Okay, I am returning by tomorrow's flight… Don't eat out, there is food in the refrigerator… hmm Bye!" Anaya disconnected the call as Olivia looked at her with a crooked look.

"What happened, Oli?"

"You disconnected the call, Mom. You never let me talk to dad. Only you talk to him…so unfair!"

"Tomorrow we are returning baby. Then you can talk to your dad all day. Don't be upset." Anaya caressed Olivia's hair when a lady dressed in black trousers and white shirt summoned Anaya from behind her.

"Yes?"

"Ma'am, can I interview you, please?" the lady pleaded.

"My mom rarely gives an interview…don't you know?" Oli said matter-of-factly.

"She is right; I don't give interviews. I am sorry," Anaya said.

"Please ma'am, we will hardly detain you here. I will take just five minutes of your time." The lady kept pleading and the cameraman moved in all directions.

"Okay, just five minutes," Anaya said and gestured Olivia to keep shut.

The interviewer told the cameraman to setup and introduced herself to Anaya as Debina, a journalist and a poet.

"Mrs. Anaya Chatterjee, who is the inspiration behind your writing?"

"Agony," Anaya replied.

"Agony? You mean pain?"

"Yes. Every human being is subjected to some kind of pain in their lifetime. The pain to which I was subjected did not break me; it inspired me to be a writer." Debina was slightly surprised.

"Wow! Amazing."

"Next question."

"Yes, who is the greatest source of support in your life?"

"My soul, for it always supports my mind. Apart from that, I have a very supportive family."

"Is any of your books based on your own life?" "All of them have some line with my life and that line is me, being a woman. As you know, all my books are based on a woman's struggle, a woman's love and her victory."

"That's very witty. What is the purpose behind your writing?" Debina knew she had little time and kept her questions direct.

"I write to ease my suffering. I write when I am hurt. I write when I am happy. Writing is my personal freedom. What I can't say I can write. Most importantly, as I said in my speech today, I write to survive."

"Suffering, pain...what is the reason behind your suffering, Mrs. Chatterjee?"

"As artists, we are eternally heartbroken and this prospect makes us successful. The suffering is inevitable for every artist, it doesn't require a reason."

"But...?" Debina tried to get into the depth of this vague answer, only to be cut in between.

"Thank you Miss Debina, good night," Anaya said conclusively and approached Olivia.

"Arrogant woman!" Debina stamped her foot.

Anaya Chatterjee never cared what people said behind her back; she was the most successful writer of this country and had been recognized in several foreign countries as well. People who flatter and claim to be your biggest fan in front of you wear another mask as soon as you turn your back. Anaya Chatterjee carried her dignity wherever she went, only to be confused with snobbery by many.

REFLECTIONS OF THE ABANDONED MIRROR

The next morning, Anaya made up her mind to visit the Kalighat Kali Temple in Kolkata which is one of the 51 shakti peethas also. Her in-laws had great faith in Goddess Kali and believed that any prayers offered to Her at the Kalighat Temple were always answered. Though Anaya knew nothing of the Bengali culture before marriage since she was a Marathi girl, her irrevocable love for Nishith and his family had made her adopt their culture. Whenever she visited Kolkata, she never forgot to visit the Kalighat Temple and offer prayers for Nishith, Olivia and Nishith's family.

Anaya was an orphan and had never seen her parents, but she had found her parents in Nishith's. They were not just her in-laws, they were her parents for whom she could sacrifice her own happiness, without complaining.

It was 8 a.m. when Anaya reached the temple. As usual, there was a large crowd of pilgrims. She felt relieved that she had not compelled Olivia to come with her as she knew her daughter would have irritated the life out of her upon seeing the seething crowd. Anaya recollected the last time she had come here with Nishith; he had persuaded her to wear the traditional white Bengali sari with a red border.

Anaya never had a fascination for saris, but to please Nishith, she wore them occasionally. She could have done anything to please Nishith. She herself wondered how, after more than twenty years of their marriage, she felt this way for him. Nishith was not only her husband, the father of her daughter, but a man with whom a lifetime spent would seem too short. Not that they fought less and had more happy moments, but because Anaya enjoyed even the fights she had with Nishith. When they fought, Anaya felt like going out of their house, never to come back. But when the effect of the fight ebbed, she laughed remembering how even after becoming parents of a daughter, now eighteen years old, they still fought like newly-weds.

She missed Nishith when she prayed in front of the image of the goddess and thought she would bring Oli with her the next time. She wanted her daughter to experience the same divine feeling which Anaya had. "Ma, I owe so much to you for giving me more than what I deserve. Always keep my Nishith and Oli healthy, give all my happiness to them. Fulfil all their dreams, let her get admitted to a nice college for the Film Studies course she wants to do and bless her with lots of success. Nishith has been nominated for the panel of world's top doctors; please let him win the best cardiologist award. Keep Ma and Baba healthy; take care of them in my absence. Give me patience and courage to face all the problems that come my way. Thanks once again Ma, for everything. Bless and protect my family, always." Saying this in her mind, Anaya opened her eyes. Though deeply spiritual, very few except Nishith had some inkling of this side of her which reflected in her writings often.

Anaya felt relaxed and an inner peace prevailed in her mind after she offered her prayers. She decided to sit for some time within the temple premises near the tank known as Kundupukur.

It had only been an hour that she had come and her flight to Singapore was at 2 p.m. Anaya sat on one of the stairs facing the sacred temple tank and got absorbed in the solitude and the spring breeze that caressed her face gently. She pondered over a lot of things, but most importantly, she thought of all the mistakes she had made in her life, intentionally or un-intentionally. Within the next few minutes, she consoled herself that it was only human to make mistakes. She tried to push aside the sword of guilt jabbing her heart when she noticed a familiar figure at the other end of the sacred temple tank. Anaya kept looking at that figure; it was a woman wearing a dowdy dress. Her face seemed very familiar to her. She wondered where she had seen her and after a minute or two, it rang a bell. She walked around the tank to the other side to have a closer view of her, and more importantly, to find out if her guess had been right. Anaya gently touched the shoulder of the woman whose face was turned away from her. As soon as she turned around, Anaya cried out, "Varsha, it's you! Oh my God, how are you?"

Anaya's eyes welled up as she recognized her cousin whom she was meeting almost two decades later. Anaya hugged her cousin, wiping those drops of tears from her face, but was taken aback when she found no response from the other side.

"Hey Varsha, didn't you recognize me? I am Anaya, your Anu…." Anaya spoke helplessly but found the same response from the other side. The lady retreated from Anaya's arms and got up from the place where she had been sitting. She carried a perplexed expression which had tints of nervousness all over.

"Varshu…why are you so scared? I am Anu, why are you going away?" Anaya shouted with frustration lined in her voice and followed Varsha. Just then, a middle-aged lady came in between.

Anaya stood like a statue when she saw Varsha hiding behind that lady so that Anaya can no longer follow her. Trapped in the whirlpool of unexpected events, Anaya heaved a deep sigh, throwing her hands in air. The lady who had just arrived came towards Anaya and started speaking, "Hello madam. I am the nurse of Howrah Mental Hospital and she is my patient. Do you know her?"

Anaya was shocked to hear that. It took her a few seconds to gather her thoughts and say, "Yes, she is my cousin. What happened to her?"

"She is a patient of Alzheimer's disease and she has been in our institution for over two years. We did not even know that her name is Varsha. We named her Maya after she was brought in." Seeing Anaya's expression change from shock to sadness in split second, she quickly added, "She is not like other mental patients. She just cannot retain any memory." The lady's revelation left Anaya speechless.

After recovering from the abrupt news, Anaya asked the nurse, "Who dropped her in your hospital?"

"Some man who had found her on the streets of Kolkata, unaware and unsure of where she wanted to go."

Anaya tried to swallow the lump that had formed in her throat and said, "Does your hospital have doctors who can treat her disease?"

"Our doctors mostly treat mentally unstable people, there are no such experts in our hospital who can treat an Alzheimer's patient. But since we didn't know anything about her or her family, we decided to keep her under our supervision till we figured a better way out." Anaya took out a pen and paper from her bag in a second and wrote her contact number and handed it to the nurse. "This is my number. Call me whenever she is not well or whenever you wish to talk to any of her family member." The nurse took the paper and the nurse nodded. "Can I get your number, please?" Anaya said anxiously.

The nurse gave her the office number of the mental hospital as well as her personal contact number, which Anaya promptly took down. Anaya looked at Varsha with sadness languished on her eyes and told the nurse, "I will call you soon." Saying this, she moved towards her car. A fountain of sadness spilled through Anaya's blood as she rushed towards her car. More than the sadness, a plethora of implacable, unrelenting guilt washed over her soul. She sat in her car, oblivious to the honking of other vehicles. All that she could hear at that particular moment were the screams of her inner voice. Her screams questioned her integrity and she looked at the rear-view mirror questioning her inner voice, "Am I responsible for Varsha's fate? What I did in the past, was that truly implacable?" Her reflection seemed to abdicate her. The long abandoned mirror pulled her into her past mistake which she had locked somewhere away from everyone, away from her own self. Destiny had unearthed that key and opened the lock, flooding her with tears of realization.

A SILENT STORM

Anaya sat in her own room, waiting for her husband's return from the hospital. Three hours had already passed after Anaya and Olivia reached home, and Olivia had gone out for her best friend's birthday bash. A whirlpool of emotions pinched Anaya's heart ever since she had met Varsha in Kolkata. Even now, when she was cosy in her house in Singapore, waiting for her husband, those disturbing thoughts did not retreat from her mind. Nishith and Anaya lived in a luxurious three bedroom apartment in Newton, an urban area within the central region of Singapore. Newton is an expensive place to live in, but the spaciousness and liberally sprinkled greenery had attracted Nishith and Anaya to choose this for their dwelling. Moreover, the handsome amount of money that Nishith made being a senior doctor of the National Heart Centre, made such luxury possible.

"I am sorry for being late, Anu. I had a last minute emergency," Nishith spoke as he saw his wife sitting in distress on the sofa of their living room. Dr. Nishith Chatterjee did not look like one of those middle-aged doctors who seem to be extremely serious and boring.A teenager would surely describe him as one of those cute and good-humoured doctors that they show in daily soaps and romantic movies: tall, handsome, dignified and a man who possessed a disarming smile. In his simple black trousers and plain lilac full shirt, he looked quite handsome; those rimless spectacles were truly a cherry on the cake. Nishith's words broke Anaya's reverie and she looked at Nishith with pale eyes.

"Your daughter is boiling at you," Anaya managed to say softly.

"Oh, where is Oli? Oli…Oli…" Nishith summoned Olivia.

"She is at Rishi's place," Anaya informed him.

"Again? I hate this guy Rishi. He is such a spoilt brat. Why did you allow Oli to go to his place, Anu?" Nishith said exhausted as he took his glasses off.

"Come on! Stop being such an over-possessive father, Nish. Rishi is a nice guy. He is our daughter's best friend and it's his birthday today. So just let Oli enjoy with him." Anaya said in a pacifying tone.

"It's not about being over possessive, it's about being caring."

"So, do you think I care for our daughter any less than you?" Anaya said raising her eye-brows.

"Oh no…not again! You win every argument we have regarding Oli."

"That is because I am a writer mummy and you are a doctor daddy. You dwell in logic land and I dwell more in the emotional land. You see, that is why I understand Oli slightly more, and trust me, she really likes Rishi's company," Anaya explained.

"What? You mean she loves him?" Nishith almost shouted out of exasperation.

"Oh God, spare me the shock! No Nish, I meant to say that Rishi is Oli's best friend and they both love and enjoy each other's company. What's bad in that?" Anaya said controlling her laughter at Nishith's panic-stricken tone.

"Bad is that I dislike Rishi. He is a spoilt brat, always up to some annoying piece of mischief," Nishith frowned.

"But our Oli is a good girl, and she will make Rishi a better guy.

Now you stop being such a hyper dad and freshen up. I have cooked your favourite butter chicken for you." Anaya said moving towards the kitchen.

"Listen, Anu..." Nishith grabbed Anaya's hand as she walked towards the kitchen.

"What? Have more complaints against that poor Rishi?" she smiled.

"Nah! Many many congratulations for your success. You are indeed the best writer this world has ever witnessed. I am so proud of you. You are not only the best writer, but also the best mother and the best wife anyone can ever have. I am indeed a lucky man." Nishith embraced Anaya and Anaya's eyes welled up at his gesture.

"Am I really a good wife and a good mother?" Anaya questioned back.

"Of course you are!" He gave her a peck on the forehead and quickly added, "So, my superwife, let me change. I am starving for the butter chicken."

Nishith went inside the bedroom leaving Anaya in a tornado of emotions. Anaya was in the midst of a silent cyclone that was waiting to take the form of a destructive storm. Anaya swallowed the whirlpool of emotions so that Nishith would feel everything was normal.

"The chicken is delicious. You were asking me whether you are a good wife, come on, I mean none of my friend's wives can cook such wonderful food, I can bet." Nishith laughed but Anaya remained wordless.

"Are you disturbed about something, Anu?"

"A little. Some of the characters of my new book are driving me crazy," she managed a faint smile. This was the excuse Anaya gave to Nishith every time he asked her whether she was stressed.

"Oh, writers' brains! Give your mind a break, at least when you are dining with your family." Nishith and Anaya shared a small round of laughter.

"Can I ask you an irrelevant question?" Anaya spoke breaking a five-minute silence.

"You can ask me anything, Anu. Stop seeking permissions."
"What will you do if you come to know that I have committed a remorseless, implacable mistake?" Anaya asked looking down into her plate, fiddling with the fork and a piece of chicken.

"Mistakes committed by loved ones can never be unforgiving or implacable, dear. The moment one realizes one's mistake and starts to repent, they no longer stay unforgiving. That's what I feel," Nishith exclaimed. Anaya merely nodded her head in response.

"I am sure this question came to your head in the course of creating a plot for your book…right?" Nishith asked.

"Yeah, exactly!" Anaya answered almost whimsically.

That night, Anaya couldn't let slumber catch her eyes. It was 2 a.m. and she sat on her bed, bewildered. It seemed every time she tried to sleep, Varsha's face came to haunt her, robbing her off her peace of mind. Anaya's truth was hidden to everyone, except her own self. A truth that had become too heavy to bear alone after meeting Varsha by chance. A truth which was erupting as countless tears of fear from Anaya's eyes. Anaya knew well that the truth which she had hidden was so dangerous that it could destroy every relation she held close. Yet the soul of a woman was praying hard to her to reveal the truth. Trapped in the quandary, Anaya switched her laptop on and opened a fresh Word document. In bold letters, she typed **THE HIDDEN LETTERS**, story of her life. Yes, her own story, which she could not hold to herself anymore; it needed to be told. She wanted all the feelings trapped inside her heart, all the thoughts somersaulting in her mind, to wear the clothes of her words. For the first time in her life, she wanted to pen down her own story for she could no longer embrace an integral truth of her life with her heart. She wanted to embellish all her thoughts, all her emotions and the truth hidden for years into words.

"I am a human and I have made mistakes; but that does not mean I am bad at heart. I have tried to be a good wife and a good mother all my life, but maybe have ended up being a selfish woman to reach here." Anaya resolved in her mind to not let her fears win over her. With that, she reminisced the first episode from where her life had taken a turn. She went twenty-four years back in time, to the day when she had first met Nishith at Varsha's house.

A WHIFF OF AROMA

It was the time when Mumbai was but Bombay, the roads were not overpopulated and there were plenty of houses and bungalows instead of apartments and shopping malls. Even the Khans had not yet debuted in Bollywood and the '80s were just about paving a way for the '90s was just about to arrive. The Bombay of 1989 was indeed very different from the congested and glamorous Mumbai of 2014. However, two things were just the same: the street food and the ever refreshing rains.

After the demise of Anaya's parents in an accident, she was raised up by her grandmother in Nagpur. Anaya had been too young to remember her mother when she lost her, but a stroke of fate on her grandmother's heart twenty years after that had deprived her of the only woman she knew for a family. It was then that the twenty-one-year-old Anaya shifted to stay with her uncle's family in West Andheri, Mumbai. Although she felt uneasy at the new house and was distressed after her grandmother's death – who she lovingly called Aaji – her cousin Varsha took all efforts to divert her mind away from the pain. Varsha made Anaya feel so comfortable and loved within just one week that Anaya looked at life with a renewed hope. Anaya took admission in St. Xavier's College for a Master's degree in English, the same college where Varsha was doing her Master's in chemistry from. Life was going slow, monotonous and stagnant for Anaya, until the day she first met Nishith.

"Anu, can you go to our neighbour Sumona's house and keep these bottles in her refrigerator?" Anaya's aunt summoned her.

"Sure!" Anaya took the three bottles filled with water and went to their neighbour's house. In those days, everyone did not have a refrigerator in their house. Having a refrigerator labelled someone as extremely rich. To store three bottles of water in the neighbour's refrigerator and retrieving them every morning was an everyday duty for Anaya. She liked visiting Sumona aunty who resembled her mom a lot, she thought. Anaya liked spending time with her and used to gossip with her for endless hours until her aunt called her. Anaya was never fond of her own aunt as she always indirectly made Anaya realize that it was not her own house and somehow she was a burden for her. Visiting Sumona aunty every morning was her daily dose of solace.

Anaya knocked the neighbour's door but there was no movement behind it for almost five minutes. Perplexed, Anaya was about to leave when suddenly an unknown guy opened the door. Anaya was a little surprised as she had never seen this guy before. In cargo pants and a red vest, he looked equally surprised. She felt a little uneasy and looked sideways knowing not whether to ask this guy about Sumona aunty or just leave. She looked at the guy's face from the corner of her eyes and found him to be really cute. She was still languishing in her thought world when the guy in front of her spoke.

"Do I know you?"

"No, I came to meet Sumona aunty," Anaya answered, nervously clutching her dupatta within her fingers.

"Oh, you came to meet Ma! She has gone to the

Siddhivinayak Temple. By the way, I have never seen you in my locality. Who are you?"

"I think I should go," Anaya said.

"Are you a bottle-thief?" The guy said and laughed at his own silly question.

"What?"

"No, you're just carrying more bottles than your hands can hold and then you are running away without revealing your identity. I thought..."

"I am Anaya, your neighbour."

"Lie! I have been living here since childhood and I have never seen you. Varsha Joshi and her parents are my neighbours." The guy smirked, bubbling with overconfidence and making Anaya angry.

"First a thief, and now a liar! What do you think of yourself? I am Varsha's cousin for your kind information," Anaya spoke in one breath.

"Now that's better. Finally you proved that you can speak," the guy smirked again, making Anaya's blood boil in anger. How can a lady like Sumona aunty have such a stupid and irritating son, she wondered.

"Don't be so angry. I am Nishith, your neighbour and Varsha's best friend. Come on in!" His smile made Anaya forget the fight instantly.

"Varshu's best friend?" she entered the house.

"Yes, Varshu hasn't told you about me, her Einstein?" The

guy said and winked. It further dropped his image in Anaya's understanding.

"Stop winking and I did not have any amount of idea that you can be Varsha's Einstein. You look so..." Anaya swallowed her words and went towards the refrigerator.

"Looks are deceptive and those that are not deceptive are not flamboyant," Nishith said confidently.

"Whatever, can I keep these bottles in the refrigerator and take the bottles which I kept there yesterday?"

"Sure, lady," Nishith said opening the door of the refrigerator.

The refrigerator must have been on de-frosting, causing some water to have seeped down to the floor. Just as Anaya went near the refrigerator, her feet slipped rapidly and she clutched on to the nearest thing – Nishith's vest. He broke the fall by catching Anaya by her waist, even as she fell over him. What hit her was the strong smell of some rich lavender fragrance. The whiff of this strong aroma and the firm grip of Nishith's arms around her was no less than a Bollywood movie scene. Anaya finally took a close look at Nishith's face which seemed so flawless according to her: charcoal eyes, sharp nose, perfectly shaped luscious red lips, and a sharp jaw line with a hint of stubble. Moreover, his fair complexion, perfect physique and the whiff of fragrance all seemed to conspire against Anaya's senses. Though it took a longer time for Anaya to take note of the situation, once she came to, she freed herself from Nishith's grip in a fraction of a second.

"Umm, I am sorry. Look I had no intention to be Veeru of Sholay; it was the water." Nishith sounded apologetic, but the smirk remained. This time, Anaya found his smile irresistible and laughed.

"I think I should leave now."

"Take the bottles, Anaya. And I am really sorry," Nishith said handing Anaya the bottles from the refrigerator.

"Thanks," Anaya took the bottles and left.

It was already evening and Anaya still could not get over the fragrance and Nishith's irresistible smile. It had really created some magic!

DRIZZLING LOVE

"Anu, where are you so lost?" Varsha asked Anaya in the evening. Anaya looked up at Varsha and started analysing for the first time how completely different they looked. While Varsha was extremely fair, roughly five feet one inch tall and a little healthy with curly hair till her shoulders; Anaya was very slim and tall, carrying a height of approx five feet seven inches, with her long, straight hair cascading till her waist. Anaya was not too fair, but dusky in a charming way. Varsha preferred to dress in bell bottom trousers and shirts to go with it, and Anaya always preferred to dress herself in suits.

She snapped out of the thought, "Lost? No, no. I was just contemplating about life and death," Anaya mumbled to herself. Anaya's mind was never occupied with a single thought, but rather a chain of thoughts which strangulated her by and by.

"Anu, I am with you. Don't over think," Varsha said clutching Anaya's hands.

"By the way, I met your Einstein today. Let me tell you he looks like a cheap goon rather than any would-be-doctor." Anaya said with a frown on her face and narrated the series of incidents that took place in the morning, carefully editing out the part when she had fallen on Nishith. She felt it too personal to share with her cousin.

"Oh come on, Anu, he is not that mean. He just has a good sense of humour and he was just pulling your leg," Varsha giggled. "Good guys don't wink, Varsha, and he thinks too much of himself. He is so impish and rowdy." Anaya distorted her face and Varsha laughed madly at her response, when suddenly the knock on the door interrupted them.

"Hello, long time Nish. You know we were just talking about you. So you came back from your grandparents' house yesterday?" Anaya had turned around to enter into her room realizing it was Nishith, but Varsha called out to her.

"Anu, where are you going?"

"Hi Anaya!" Nishith smiled at Anaya which made Anaya stop and respond.

"Ahem! By the way Nishith, Anu was talking about you a lot. She really was impressed by you," Anaya put her hand on her forehead to hide the embarrassment that her cousin was causing to her by lying so confidently.

"Woah, really? I thought your cousin hated me at first sight," Nishith smirked and Anaya noticed it from the corner of her eyes.

"Why? What did you do that she will hate you?" Varsha interrogated and Anaya felt like cutting Varsha's curls out of anger.

"Actually your sister slipped today, and I saved her the fall," Varsha went speechless.

"Anu, you did not tell me this!" Varsha was out at teasing her now, and Anaya wanted to murder Nishith.

"I must have forgotten," Anaya lied bluntly.

"Oops! You forgot? We met just today and you forgot our first meeting so soon, Anu?" Nishith winked.

"First of all, you stop winking. And secondly, only Varsha can call me Anu. You better call me Anaya. Got it?" Anaya sniffed.

"Alright, Miss Anaya Joshi. Oh, I am sorry...Anu," Nishith and Varsha laughed out loud and Anaya went into the other room out of exasperation.

***

Even two months after this fateful first and second meeting, Anaya's vexation towards Nishith did not ebb. Anaya felt a strange rage towards Nishith. Although she hated Nishith for the way he winked at her and his all time smirking and happy-go-lucky nature, she was enraged because these very things attracted her to him. Nishith was a very bright student of The Grand Medical Hospital who had higher ambitions of becoming a very successful cardiologist.

There was an annual function in St Xavier's college and Varsha compelled Nishith to watch her dance performance. Since Anaya usually spent time with Varsha, and hadn't made any other good friends in the short time-span yet, she was a little pacified on seeing Nishith to give her company in the audience.

"Why aren't you performing something, Anu?" Nishith asked Anaya as he sat on the chair beside her in the audience.

"That's none of your business. And please call me Anaya, not Anu."

"You sing so well, you should have at least sung a song," Nishith said in a serious tone, looking straight at Anaya's eyes.

"Now when have you heard me sing?"

"Come on, Anu! You are my neighbour and our rooms are exactly opposite each other's. So whatever you do, I have count of all those things," Nishith smirked. Anaya almost got tired of forbidding Nishith to call her Anu.

"You obnoxious creature! You don't feel ashamed to stalk me? You are just so shameless," Anaya said raising her eyebrows.

Nishith was about to speak something but Varsha's name was announced and both of them looked at the stage with transfixed eyes as Varsha danced to a medley of famous Bollywood numbers She looked extremely pretty wearing that signature colourful skirt, that tiara on her head like Madhuri Dixit's outfit in the song 'ek, do, teen...'. Both Nishith and Anaya applauded watching Varsha's moves and Nishith started whistling at the end of Varsha's performance.

"Has anyone told you yet that more than a future in the medical world, you have a possible golden future in the world of goons?" Anaya said with exasperation as she saw Nishith whistling loudly after the performance.

"Oh Anu, you are a doll. I just love the way you sniff every time you scold me."

"Oh god! Why do I even talk to you? You are a walking talking annoy bug, do you know that?" Anaya said and left the auditorium. Just then, her head started spinning and she felt dizzy. A dark air of smoke clouded her eyes and she fell down in the middle of the auditorium.

When Anaya opened her eyes, it was midnight. Varsha was sleeping beside her and Anaya wondered how she had come there and what had happened to her in the evening.

While Anu struggled to wear her slippers and get up from the bed, Varsha woke up rubbing her eyes, "Anu, how are you feeling now?"

"I am better. What happened to me?"

"I don't know, Nishith said you had low blood pressure and fainted. He carried you here and was extremely perturbed by your condition. He was feeling guilty that since he was annoying you, you left the auditorium and fell down. Anyway, after he brought you here, he measured your blood pressure and it was very low. He has prepared a diet chart for you and prescribed some vitamins. You will be perfectly fine if you follow them, Anu." Anu was looking at her confused, it was way too much to process in one go. Varsha continued nonetheless, "Oh, and while you fell, your. head hit the side of a chair and there was a small cut and little blood loss. Nishith bandaged your head, so don't worry at all." Varsha hugged Anaya, comforting her. Anaya was really moved by Nishith's concern for her. She had thought Nishith to be an extremely careless guy but from what Varsha had just told her, her perception of Nishith was changed. 'Looks are deceptive,' Anaya recollected Nishith's words and smiled. She herself did not realize when she slept thinking of Nishith that night.

The next morning was rainy. Bombay rains don't follow any season and this was one such day when rains seemed to be an uninvited and uninformed visitor. Anaya's sleep was interrupted by the drizzle of rain which effortlessly crept up to her face through the open window.

She was wondering where Varsha was when she heard, "Good morning, Anu. Have this glass of milk."

"I need tea. It is such a lovely rainy morning and you are giving me a glass of milk. You know how much I hate milk. Remember by M3 phobia… milk, mathematics and monkeys." Anaya said making a puppy face.

"You have to drink this milk, Anaya." Anaya felt a little surprised to hear Anaya instead of Anu from Nishith who came in right after Varsha.

"I hate milk," she persisted.

"You have to follow this diet chart, Anaya. I am your doctor now and you have to listen to me," Nishith said in a serious tone and Anaya was surprised to see the guy who used to annoy the grey matter out of her brains talking in such a decent doctor-like manner. Anaya did not argue and had the milk in one sip, crumbling her tiny nose.

"Excellent. That's like a good girl," Nishith spoke and gave the empty glass to Varsha who went towards the kitchen to keep it. "Nishith…" Anaya got up from the bed and went towards the window where Nishith was standing.

"What happened?"

"Thanks for all the help yesterday. Varsha told me everything."

"Sorry for annoying you too much, Anu…I mean Anaya."

"It's okay and listen, you can call me Anu."

Nishith raised his eyebrows in surprise.

"Friends?" Anaya extended her right hand towards Nishith which he promptly took into his.

HEARTBEAT

Winter in Bombay was not as bone-chilling as Calcutta or Delhi. Nishith and Anaya had become really good friends in the four months that had past. The three friends – Varsha, Nishith and Anaya – now had a weekly tradition of going to the Juhu beach to enjoy street food. They had pani puri, wada pav and ragda patties (all spicy and delicious vegetable street food of Bombay) together and talked a lot about each other's lives. The conversation often revolved around Anaya since Nishith and Varsha knew each other well from childhood. Anaya found in her Varshu and Nish trustworthy companions and shared her deepest feelings with them without restraint. She also shared with them her secret dream of becoming a writer one day.

It was one such fine evening when they had been talking about Anaya's undergoing so much pain when Aaji passed away.

"I am so lucky to get you both!" Anaya held their hands in each of hers, looking at rising and crashing of the tides.

"We are lucky too! You know, Anu, you are like these waves yourself. No matter how many times life has knocked you down, you always managed to stand up on your feet. Mark my words: you will be very successful one day and the whole world will know you," Nishith said with a gleam of confidence in his eyes.

"Exactly Nish, you know Anaya writes so well. You must check her diary, the poems and short stories she scribbles there.... I am speechless. One day, you will definitely become a writer, Anu," Varsha hugged Anaya saying those words.

"By the way, when will you show me your diary? I so want to read it," Nishith said as the sisters hugged each other.

"Let's go home now and you can read it," Varsha suggested and Anaya nodded her head too.

The three of them landed home and Nishith started reading Varsha's diary voraciously until he paused on one of the poems and started reading it loudly.

Love me like you love a feather

Because I am too fragile and subtle;

Love me like you love an old song

So that you can hum me at midnight when you are lost in your thoughts;

Love me like you love a rose

So that you don't regret when I get dry and perish;

Love me like you love the first drop of rain

Because I want to comfort you first after the burning heat has tormented you;

Love me like you love the moon

Because it will be enchanting for me whenever you will gaze at me;

Love me like you love the morning breeze

So that I can caress you gently after you open your eyes;

Love me like you love the word "Love"

Sublime, pure and so divine;

I will love you like I love my own Life

Just want to whisper you these ten words before I die!

"Wow Anu, the man who will get your love will be very lucky," Nishith said in an enchanting tone after reading the poem and Varsha applauded.

"I told you Nish she writes so well," Varsha smiled.

"Come on! This is just a rough poem which I had casually scribbled one day," Anaya said softly.

"But it was overflowing with feelings. Have you ever fallen in love with someone?" Nishith asked Anaya abruptly.

"Me? No…never. Have you ever loved someone?" Anaya looked at him curiously.

"Will tell you some other day," Nishith winked.

"Not fair, you have to tell us right now!" Varsha screamed.

"Okay Varshu, why don't you start? You tell us if you have ever fallen in love," Anaya was taken aback when Nishith began laughing like a lunatic.

"I don't believe in love, and Nish, stop laughing. I will kill you." Varsha started throwing pens and pencils kept in the pen stand on Nishith's head and the tidy room changed into an utter mess within ten minutes.

"Okay, now you two, stop fighting!" Anaya finally jumped in.

"By the way, I have a surprise for you two. Tomorrow we are

going to watch the movie *Maine Pyar Kiya*. I have already bought the tickets for the first day first show; don't be late!" Nishith said combing his messed up hair with his pocket comb.

"Wow Nish, thank you. I just love the hero of this movie, he is so cute. I saw the posters, I have a huge crush on him," Varsha jumped out of joy.

"Yeah, what's his name...Salman Khan! The heroine is cute too.then we will be on time, I guess," Nishith said and waved goodbye to the sisters.

The three went to Maratha Mandir and had a wonderful time watching the movie. While Varsha was busy munching popcorn and gazing at her new crush Salman, Anaya was in tears after every sentimental scene and Nishith was the handkerchief supplier to Anaya at such times.

"Wow, the movie was so romantic," Anaya said as they had kulfi after coming out of the hall.

"Some scenes were too funny though, too dramatic. That dialogue, 'Ek ladka aur ladki kabhi dost nahi ho sakte...' – a girl and a guy can never be best friends – was so illogical," Varsha spoke.

"Have one more kulfi Varshu; it will cool you down," Nishith laughed.

"Shut up! One more kulfi in this winter will give me a sore throat. Anu, you tell me, am I right or not? If the dialogue writers knew the three of us and our friendship, they wouldn't have incorporated such a silly dialogue in the movie," Varsha continued.

Anaya sniffed and nodded her head in response.

"What I liked in the movie was Salman Khan. He is so cute and the songs are awesome," Varsha was totally in love with her newfound crush.

"Even that romantic song on the terrace...wow," Anaya said lost in thoughts.

"I agree," Nishith said.

The next evening, Anaya went to Nishith's house to give a box full of kanda pohe (a Marathi snack) prepared by her aunt, which she knew Nishith loved. Nishith was a Bengali, and did not get to eat a lot of Marathi cuisine in his house. So whenever Varsha's mom cooked kanda pohe or wada pav, she always sent some for Nishith. As Anaya approached Nishith's room after handing the box to Sumona aunty, she could hear the same song from *Maine Pyar Kiya* playing in the tape recorder that she had mentioned the previous day.

Wow you have this cassette! Today I am going to borrow this cassette from you. I so darn love the songs of this movie, "especially…" Nishith interrupted Anaya and completed her sentence. "*Mere rang mein rangne wali*…I know. Since you are such a romantic soul."

Anaya blushed.

"Do you know the theme of this song is taken from Andy William's Where Do I begin (Love Story)? The English version is far more romantic than this one. It is one of the most romantic songs I have ever heard. Well, let me make you hear it." Nishith said and changed the cassette and a wonderful melodious song started playing. Anaya got enthralled and captivated in the song and Nishith asked for her hand to dance. Anaya refused a couple of times but gave in to Nishith's words the third time.

Nishith wrapped his arm around her waist and Anaya clutched his shoulder. As the song played on, Anaya began losing herself. She could hear nothing but her own heartbeat, getting louder. When Nishith held her right hand with his left hand and pulled her a little close to him by her waist, Anaya felt a mild current run down her. She withdrew herself from Nishith on impulse and sat on the chair. Anaya could feel her heart thumping very loud, to her own surprise.

"What happened, Anu?" The doctor in Nishith woke up observingAnaya's strange behaviour.

"Nothing... It's just that I have never danced with a guy, so felt a little nervous."

"Come on, we are friends. You don't need to feel embarrassed with me. You remember asking me yesterday if I have ever loved someone? After reading your poem and after thinking about your question all night yesterday, I feel that I have started feeling for someone, someone very special," Nishith said with a spark of happiness in his face.

"Who is it? Did you tell her yet?" Anaya asked, curious, her heart beating harder now.

"No way! I am not going to tell her. What if she doesn't feel the same way for me?" Nishith laughed.

"I doubt any girl will refuse you, Nish. By the way, you can tell me who she is," Anaya asked mustering some courage and biting her lip out of angst.

"Can't tell her name. You keep guessing," Nishith said and smirked.

Anaya came to her house and kept thinking of Nishith's

words. She wondered why she felt so restless thinking of Nishith that night. Had she really started feeling for Nishith? Was Nishith giving her hints today that it was her he had started feeling for? All these thoughts were somersaulting in Anaya's head. The one thing she was sure of was: she really liked Nishith from the core of her heart. She was not sure if it could be called love; it could have been mere infatuation. But she knew for sure that she would like it immensely if she was the girl Nishith was talking about.

COLOUR ME, MY LOVE!

The butterflies in her stomach and a secret coyness refrained Anaya from making any efforts to dig the secret out of Nishith's heart, especially without being sure of her strong semblance towards Nishith. Slowly and steadily, Anaya realized that Nishith possessed her soul. He had captivated her senses and conquered her heart. Nishith was a man she could spend endless hours with and still not tire. He made Anaya blush; his supple and amorous touches (though a very few, which left her wanting for more) made her heart sing every unsung song that a person madly in love can only experience.

"Anu, do you have something for Nishith?" Varsha asked Anaya after dinner one day when Anaya was scribbling something in her diary with a dreamy look on her face.

"Uh what?" Anaya retorted fixing her eyes on her diary.

"Stop being pretentious, for heaven's sake! I have seen that stealthy look on your face every time you look at Nish." Varsha said snatching Anaya's diary.

"Stop it, Varsha!"

"You stop it, Anu! If you can't tell me, then how will you tell Nish?" Varsha winked naughtily.

"Why can't he tell me?" Anaya said and bit her lip realizing what she had just said.

"Ah ha! There you go!" Varsha said raising her eyebrows.

Anaya buried her face in Varsha's shoulders out of the impetuous embarrassment she just caused to herself.

"Come on, Anu! I am so happy about you and Nish...you both will have the most good-looking kids on this planet," Varsha said hugging Anaya.

"Kids? I am not even sure if Nishith loves me..." Anaya paused. What if he does not feel the same way for me at all?

"How can someone not love you, Anu? You are just too perfect as a woman. I mean, just look at you! Your long, lustrous hair, this tender shyness and the lovable smile can melt any man's heart in a second." Varsha said ushering Anaya's hair in order to tease her.

"Now you are making me nervous, Varshu!!" Anaya said cupping her face with both her hands.

"Hey Anu, should I tell Nishith about your feelings for him in case you feel too shy to tell him?"

"Hell, no! Swear on me you won't do such a terrible thing!" Anaya jumped out of the bed.

"Okay Anu, chill! I won't tell Nish a word about you, but you promise me that you will convey your feelings to him as soon as possible."

"Alright! I will try."

"Tomorrow is Holi. Why not give him some hint about your feelings?" Varsha suggested with child-like expression.

"You always come up with some plan on the other. I am very sleepy, let me sleep now!" Anaya switched off her bedside lamp and pondered about Nishith when her lips broke into a smile.

The next morning was a brighter day for Anaya: she was peppier at the prospect of Holi with Nish and Varsha; the spring breeze made the whole setting very romantic. The cumulus clouds were playing hide and seek with the sun and all around, people with colour-packed faces were sharing smiles and laughter. The aura of the festival was spreading fast and it soon reached Anaya's heart as well. It kept pounding every now and then, thinking of her love.

Anaya draped herself in a sleeveless white chikan salwar kameez and a red white bandhani dupatta which made her reflection in the mirror look envious. After offering her prayers to Lord Krishna and adorning Lord Krishna's idol with gulal, Anaya made her way towards the ground where people from their locality assembled to play Holi. She saw Nishith from a distance, dressed in a white kurta and white trouser, talking to an old woman. White made Nishith look so exceptionally handsome that Anaya could not even realize when Nishith's mom, Sumona aunty tapped her shoulders.

"Aunty? Happy Holi!" Anaya touched her feet immediately.

"Happy Holi Anu...let me put some colour on your face." She lovingly touched her colour-smeared fingers on her cheeks and added, "Yes, now you are looking prettier. How I wish I had a daughter like you!"

"You remind me so much of my Mom, aunty," Anaya said and her eyes welled up with emotions.

"Why don't you just call me Maa? I have always pined for a daughter after I gave birth to a stillborn daughter so many years back. God blessed me with Nishith, but the agony of separation from my daughter never left my soul. You know Anu, I even decided her name when I was pregnant. I was about to name her

Olivia, but fate had other plans!" She looked up at Anu again who was visibly upset at her overflowing emotions, and quickly gathered herself, "Just look at me, I am boring you with my life's story, that too on a festival. I am sorry." Sumona said wiping her tears behind her spectacles.

"You don't need to feel sorry aunty…I mean Mom…" The bond had been etched in both the hearts now, "The way you pined for a daughter your whole life, I pined for a mother's love since childhood. I am so lucky that I met you. You provide such deep solace to my heart." Anaya said unable to hide the plethora of emotions that washed over her, and hugged her.

Sumona took Anaya in her arms and assured her that she will be with Anaya in every bright and dark situation that she will face thereafter.

After she had left to greet others from the neighbourhood, Anaya's eyes once again searched for Nishith. Soon, she saw Nishith hugging Varsha tightly from the back and forcibly applying colours all over her face; Varsha was screaming loudly. At first, Anaya laughed, but a second glimpse made her feel uncomfortable. Nishith's left hand was wrapped around Varsha's waist and his lips uttered something near Varsha's ears. Anaya felt as if something pricked her deep down. A silent wind of innocent jealousy touched Anaya, making her look away. Anaya was still thinking about the scene when suddenly Varsha's shriek very close to her broke her thoughts.

"Anu, I would have murdered your Nishith. Just look what that devil has done!" Varsha said, pointing towards her face which resembled that of a joker now. Anaya forgot all else and broke into laughter.

"Why did you spare him? You should have also given it back to him," Anaya said controlling her laughter.

"I couldn't reach his face, Anu. He is too tall for me, you know. Can you please do me a favour?" Varsha said with a grin and whispered something in Anaya's ears.

"Hey Nish, Happy Holi!" Anaya said. Nishith turned around to face her and kept looking at her without saying a word.

"What?" Anaya said after a few seconds of silence, feeling slightly uncomfortable under Nishith's magnetic gaze.

"You look so pretty that I was thinking how to make this faceprettier with colours." Nishith's words ran a tickling sensation over Anaya's body as she thought how it will be when Nishith will touch Anaya's face with an excuse of Holi. Anaya blushed lowering her eyelashes when Nishith took two handfuls of red colour from the plate and applied them on Anaya's cheeks gently, making Anaya crave for more of his touch. He then took two handfuls of green colour from another plate and applied on the rest of the face and neck with supple tenderness, which made Anaya feel as if the colour had made its way directly to her heart. Her lips broke into a shy smile of satisfaction.

"You look beautiful!" Nishith said as he looked at Anaya, coloured all over.

"Can I?" Anaya lifted her hands with colours, after regaining her senses from Nishith's touch.

"Sure, lady!" Nishith said.

"Close your eyes!" Anaya ordered.

"Why?"

"Just for me, please," she cooed.

Nishith smiled and closed his eyes. As soon as he did that, Anaya poured a bucket full of red water on him with Varsha's help, making Nishith give out a cry of unexpected shock. Anaya started laughing at his response and Varsha shrieked in excitement, "Why smarty? How was it?"

Nishith started laughing too, watching the two ladies giggle out of triumph.

"I didn't know this naughty side of you, Anu. You are a chamber of secrets," Nishith said while Anaya and he were walking back home.

"Even you have a whole lot of secrets hidden behind. I still did not get to know about the girl you are in love with. At least give her some hint, even if you don't tell me about her," Anaya said looking at Nishith.

"Do you really think I should give her some hint?" Nishith asked.

"I think you should." Her heart was ready to bounce out of her chest as she looked at Nishith.

"What would you have done had you been in my place?" Nishith asked again.

"I would have waited for a signal, some hint," Anaya blushed.

"Holy Jesus! I am doing the same right now!"

THE MISUNDERSTANDING

It was deep into the dark night, about 2 a.m. and Anaya was unblinkingly staring at the open window of her room. Though the curtains were drawn, Anaya could see Nishith's shadow holding a book in the window right opposite hers. Varsha was fast asleep, maybe dancing somewhere in her dreamland. Anaya kept looking at Nishith's shadow with forlorn eyes. She felt sad and desperate as she followed his shadow. An unknown sadness engulfed her heart. *Since childhood, all I have faced is separation from all my loved ones...will Nishith be mine all my life or is it all a part of my hallucination? Anaya's heart whispered softly amidst the darkness of the night.* She said a silent prayer and fell asleep, hugging Nishith's thoughts in her heart.

Next morning, Anaya told Varsha about her conversation with Nishith where he had told her he was also waiting for a signal from the one he loved, just like Anaya. Varsha got hysterical and prodded Anaya to confess her feelings for Nishith immediately.

"Nope Varshu, I can't!" Anaya said, applying the cherry coloured nail paint on her long, shapely finger nails.

"I wonder why Nish is waiting for your signal...Be a man, Einstein!" Varsha murmured, distorting her face, when suddenly a crumpled piece of paper fell on the windowsill from outside.

It seemed someone had intentionally thrown it. Varsha picked it up immediately and read.

I know we are friends...

But I've crossed the thin line that differentiates friendship and love...

And strangely, I am not sorry! Should I be?

-Yours Nish

"Oh my God! Anu, he proposed to you! Woah!" Varsha screamed as she finished reading the few words written on that crumpled piece of paper. Anaya took the piece of paper and read it again and again, blushing uncontrollably.

"What will I do now?" Anaya asked Varsha with slightly trembling lips that kept flashing an ecstatic smile time and again.

"Tell him that he does not need to feel sorry. That you want exactly the same!" Varsha said hugging Anaya.

"I have just applied nail paint. Will you please write on my behalf on the opposite side of this paper?" Anaya said with shimmering eyes.

Varsha nodded her head and wrote exactly the words which Anaya dictated to her.

Yes, you should be SORRY!

Not for crossing the line, but for making me wait to hear

Those magical words I have been pining for!

Varsha threw the crumpled piece of paper towards Nishith's room and it landed directly where it was intended to. Varsha and

Anaya waited excitedly and after an impatient wait of a few minutes, another piece of paper flew into their window. Varsha started reading.

I am dying to whisper those words in your ear

Just a little more wait dear

At my home, 6 p.m. sharp... I will wait.

"Oh wow! Now this is too filmy, Anu," Varsha said with a naughty wink.

"Don't know what's happening inside my stomach, but my heart beats are dancing so much that I could faint. Hush! I won't go to his house at 6 p.m. No way!" Anu said, covering her face with her hands, as she felt a tickling sensation of Nishith's lips whispering in her ears.

"Shut up! I am going to dress you up today. You will look your best, Anu. Nish will faint when he sees you," Varsha grinned from ear to ear.

"If he will faint, then who will whisper those words in my ear?" Anaya smiled.

"Ah ha! There you go! Sinking, sinking, drinking water...I won't go to his house!" Varsha copied Anaya's remarkable expression and the two sisters rolled onto the bed. Nishith could also hear them giggling and felt happy that his sudden proposal was not treated as offence. He waited for the clock to strike 6 and so did Anaya.

Varsha began dressing her sister up and used kohl and eye liner on Anaya's lovely eyelids to make her eyes look delicately beautiful. She pleated her long hair with beads. The fitting red suit and churidar complimented Anaya's wheatish complexion and black hair, making her look very pretty. After Varsha was done, she hugged Anaya.

"I am the luckiest girl in the world. Two of my favourite persons are in love with each other...my best friend and my sister."

"Thanks for everything, Varshu. If you were not there, I would have never met Nishith," Anu said, teary eyed. Varsha could understand Anu's feelings but she wiped the teardrops on the verge of falling and smacked Anaya for messing up with the make-up. Just as Anaya was about to step out of her house, all lights went off.

She made her way to Nishith's house but the drum roll of her heartbeats did not fail to give her jitters. Anaya saw that the main door of Nishith's house was left open and wondered if it was for her. But it was dark inside, thanks to the power cut. After some hesitation, she entered the living room. There was no light except from the candle kept on the dining table. Anaya stood near the dining table, her eyes searching frantically for Nishith. After a minute or two, Anaya felt arms sliding around her waist and immediately recognized Nishith's touch. The flickering candle extinguished when a slight breeze swept in from the open door. It was dark all around and Nishith's arms entwined Anaya's waist lovingly. The moment was so special for Anaya that her lips could not give way to a single word, only her heart spoke through the racing heartbeats. Nishith removed his hands from her waist and held her fingers into his. After waiting for eternity, Nishith whispered into Anaya's ears.

"I love you dear, I love you so much. I don't know when it happened. You are the one who makes me feel alive; you are my best friend, my life, my everything. I know you are stupid when it comes to such stuff, you feel romance is not for you, and you fight with me every now and then. But I still love you. *I love you so much Varsha."*

Anaya's senses came crashing back to her when she heard the last word. Her eyes watered at the thought of what had just happened and a wave of perplexed emotions washed upon her. She turned towards Nishith gently. He had barely seen the tears glistening in the dark when his smile vanished. The room was flooded with light suddenly, the power was back! Both Anaya and Nishith were dumbstruck - *how and why did this happen?*

CHAIN OF EVENTS

"Anu, you...I mean, I told Varsha to be here this evening...I mean...Stop crying...Sorry..." Nishith uttered unfinished sentences, knowing not what to say or how to react.

"Nishith...you and Varsha...I am sorry," that's all Anaya could manage. She swallowed the rest of her words with the lump in her throat. Nishith loved Varsha, not her.

"Why did you come here today?" Nishith asked with a stern tone. "I...I thought...I am sorry, Nish," Anaya broke into tears once again and rushed out of the house. She bumped into Sumona outside the house, but couldn't hide her tears. Without saying a word to her, Anaya rushed inside her house and then into her room. Once she entered her room, she locked it and exploded into uncontrollable tears. Hugging her pillow and sitting on the floor, she wept like a small child. She couldn't realize what jabbed her heart more: the fact that Nishith did not love her, or the guilt that she came between Nishith and Varsha. She was anxious to know if Varsha had similar feelings for Nishith. She wanted to ask Nishith the reason he gave her all those hints in the first place.

She felt enraged, betrayed, guilty, sad and loneliness – all together – and did not know how to overcome the multiple emotions. Varsha and her aunt kept banging the door and after almost an hour, Anaya unlocked it.

"What happened with Nishith?" A worried Varsha asked her.

"He loves you, not me," Anu uttered these words with difficulty. Her aunt heard this too and understood the entire scenario involving her daughter, her not-so-affectionate niece, and the boy she considered her son ever since she could remember.

"What's new in that! Everyone in our colony knows well that Nishith and Varsha love each other since childhood...how could you even think that Nishith loves you?" Before Varsha could speak, her mother rubbed salt to Anaya's wounds.

Anaya stood there like a statue, unable to recover from the sudden shock of Nishith's confession and now this sudden blame.

"Aayi, it's not true. I don't love Nishith and neither had I known earlier that he feels this way for me. His body language and behaviour always indicated that he loves Anu," Varsha said, pacifying her mother.

"Chachi is right, Varsha. I am sorry for coming between you and Nishith. You people gave me shelter at your house after Aaji's death and I have hurt all of you, though unintentionally, with this confusion," Anaya somehow controlled her tears and uttered with a straight face.

Varsha's mother made no effort to pacify the girl who was struggling with her emotions, and kept looking at Anaya with such disgust that she felt if only the ground beneath her could swallow her for eternity. *What is the requirement of this worthless life when I have nothing to deal in life but separation? Am I not worthy of being loved and treasured by anyone?* Anaya's thoughts came to a halt when Nishith entered their room.

"Look Varsha, I need to talk to you," Nishith said, looking directly at Varsha.

"Yes Varsha, go and talk to Nishith in the other room," Varsha's mother suggested confidently and Varsha, though unwilling, moved to the next room. The rest of the night passed but three people had come to stay in just one moment. Anaya's tears kept spilling down her eyes and all

Varsha's attempts to talk to her were in vain. The next morning, when Anaya woke up, she saw Varsha smiling at her.

"Good morning, Anu."

"Morning, Varsha."

"Listen, I talked to Nishith yesterday. I am sure he is just attracted towards me because we have been together for quite a few years. And I don't think I can ever feel that way for him; I even told him this," Varsha spoke with a smile.

"So you rejected his proposal?" Anaya sounded uninterested now.

"Yes, but Aayi thinks I am doing all this for you, sacrificing my love and all that. But you know the truth…right? I don't love him," Varsha said in a clarifying tone.

"Doesn't matter, anyway. He loves you and I think you should not break his heart," Anaya said after a sigh.

"How can I love someone who has broken my dear sister's heart, Anu? Impossible task!" Anaya looked up at Varsha and sat there numb, while the latter added, "Oh, and it is against sister rules."

"Love is beyond any rules or realms. If it is for me that you have rejected Nishith, then please don't worry about me. I know Nishith doesn't love me, my sole happiness will be to be freed from the guilt that I came between you and him."

The next few days were worse. Nishith tried his best to communicate with Varsha who hardly talked to him. Never even once did Nishith try to speak to Anaya, nor did Anaya expect him to do so anyway. Varsha's mother ensured to rub Anaya's wounded heart the wrong way, more out of anxiety than jealousy. Anaya found it very difficult to face all of this together, and made up her mind to leave her uncle's house and shift to their college hostel. She hoped for things to fall in place for Nishith and Varsha and for her aunt to be happy. By going away from all this mess that had been created because of her to begin with, she thought Nishith would smile again, even if it meant sacrificing every bit of her own happiness and all that she had in the name of a family.

Finally after two weeks of planning and persuading her uncle and Varsha, Anaya was all set to shift to her college hostel.

***

"Anu, where are you going?" Mrs. Chatterjee asked Anaya as she stepped out of her uncle's house with two suitcases.

"College hostel, aunty," she managed a fake smile and explained politely, "After whatever has happened between me and Nishith, I can't stay here any longer. I will just be creating more problems and tension."

"First of all, call me Mom, not aunty. I didn't know a small misunderstanding could change that between you and me." Anaya's eyes welled up as Mrs. Chatterjee continued, "Secondly, I know well that the entire confusion has been created because of my Nishith. He misled you, gave you wrong hints and ultimately broke your heart. He has made you stand guilty today, of something that you did not do. Even I believed Nishith loves you, Anu, all this while. Being Nishith's mother, if I got misled, then it's too natural for you to have gotten confused beta. I am so sorry for what happened."

"Please don't be sorry, Mom. I will miss you," Anaya said, sobbing silently.

"You will miss me when I will let you go." Anaya looked up, confused. "From today on, you will stay with me, in my house," Mrs. Chatterjee declared.

"How is that possible, Mom? You don't have to do this, really. I am fine."

"I have made my decision, Anu. Whatever Nishith has done to your life, the mess he has caused to your life, only he can improve that.....by marrying you. And he will have to," Mrs. Chatterjee said sternly.

"Mom, Nishith loves Varsha. I don't want to force him into anything."

"He has to, Anu! It's his doing, all this trouble for you."

Mrs. Chatterjee held Anaya's arm and to Varsha's delight and her mother's anger, took her home with her. Nishith was angry and very reluctant to do what his mother was asking him to. He had not even completed his MBBS, and most importantly, he did not love Anaya. The morning broke the peace in the neighbourhood after years when everyone heard Nishith's raised voice, Anaya's pleas to Mrs. Chatterjee and the lady's final cry as she fell down, unconscious.

Nishith glowered at Anu in anger, blaming her for his mother's condition. Nishith checked her pulse, and realised it was running. She had been a hypertension patient anyway and he knew he couldn't risk her life for this fight. He promised her that he would consider her proposal, but he needed to complete his MBBS first.

Nishith shifted into his college hostel and Anu lived with Mrs. Chatterjee, taking good care of her. Nishith, in the meantime arranged to meet Varsha so as to talk it out with her. He met a dead end when the girl who he could do anything for turned him away, blaming him for all the unhappiness her sister had to go through. In the restlessness and anxiety of having fallen so low in his love's eyes, and more owing to his mother's health and happiness, he said yes. He continued staying in the hostel, completely cut off from his family and Varsha's and completed his MBBS as Anaya completed her Master's degree and began working. Amidst such circumstances, Nishith's maternal uncle suggested to Mrs. Chatterjee that Anaya and Nishith should marry and live away from the circumstances that had killed such a beautiful bond between them. Since he himself was a well-known doctor in Singapore, he spoke to Nishith about a post doctoral in Cardiology from a well-known institute and offered help.

Nishith's heart had been broken too, he was too numb to feelings now. So, at Mrs. Chatterjee's insistence and in a ceremony with not more than twenty odd people from both families, Nishith and Anaya got married. They were to fly to Singapore immediately after that. But the distance remained, physical, mental, emotional.

Anaya felt pained at the thought of being married to a boy who didn't love her, and more at the thought of leaving her Godmother, her mother-in-law, her sunshine in days of fog, Mrs. Sumona Chatterjee.

And the day before they had to leave, Anaya broke down. "Mom, I can't bear to stay away from you. Nishith doesn't love me, not even as a friend now. I can spend a hundred years with you and Papa, happily. An orphan like me could feel the love of parents for the first time. How will I survive there? Nishith will never love me, Mom. He thinks I have separated him from his love," Anaya said wiping her tears.

Mrs. Chatterjee was calm, "You are the one for Nishith, Anu. Varsha might have been his first love, but you are his true love. And one day Nishith will realize this. Your love will make him forget Varsha forever. Be with him, shower him with all your love and I guarantee you that your love will no longer stay unrequited or unanswered. Trust me." Mrs. Chatterjee said running her fingers in Anaya's hair, and the confidence in her voice gave Anaya courage.

"Really Mom? Is that possible?" Anaya said, looking at her mother-in-law.

"Yes Anu. Just never get tired of expressing your love to Nishith. He will realize one day your true value in his life, and when he does, he will love you madly." She stopped and looked out the window, "Can you see that banyan tree?"

Anaya nodded her head in response.

"You are like that banyan tree. Nishith watches you every day and thinks that it is due to your presence that rose shrubs could not grow longer. But one day when the sun will shine bright at him and he will long for a shade, he will run to you. He will then realize your worth and the reason you came into his life. Just never give up, beta...promise me, you won't," Mrs. Chatterjee said holding Anaya's hands.

"I promise Mom. And I love you so much," Anaya hugged her.

Soon after, Nishith and Anaya flew to Singapore to start the new chapter of their life. Anaya resolved to not give up loving Nishith ever, no matter what happened. Nishith was her love, and now her husband and her life.

THE YEARS LONG GONE

"Anu, get up! It's 9 a.m.!" Nishith's voice woke Anaya up and she realized within a fraction of second that she had slept in the study while working on her own story last night. Anaya opened her drowsy eyes and looked at the tray kept in front – two cups of steaming tea with some cookies. She saw Nishith smiling at her, just like a parent does for a child.

"Nish, you should have woken me up earlier. Why did you…?" Anaya said with a glint of smile on her face.

"I know we have been married for two decades now, but that doesn't mean I can't make tea for my loving, hardworking wife," Nishith said as he sat on the chair right opposite hers.

"You are such an endearing husband. I pray to God every single day that our Oli gets someone like you in her life," Anaya said sipping her morning tea, which for her, this was the best tea of the world.

"She will get a better man than me; I will ensure that. But youare much lucky in this case…aren't you?" Nishith raised up his eyebrows.

"Of course, Dad! Mom is super lucky to get you and so are you …the best-looking couple I have ever seen," Olivia said, entering the study room.

"Oli, were you eavesdropping your parents' conversation from the corner of the room?" Anaya asked.

"Come on, Anu. Oli is a big lady now; she can hear her parents' conversations and even be a part of them," Nishith defended his adorable daughter.

"Exactly! Dad is always right," Olivia hugged Nishith.

"How did you wake up so early, by the way, young lady?" Anaya interrogated again.

"I have lots of work to do Mom. Be ready for a surprise guys," Olivia said, smiling naughtily.

"Oh boy, I can smell something fishy!" Anaya murmured.

"Our daughter is planning some surprise for us and you are being so investigative!" Nishith seemed excited, "Let's wait and see what it is!"

"I love you two!" Olivia chirped, "Okay I got to go. You people carry on with your morning romance....oops sorry," Olivia bit her lower lip and left the study.

"This girl has become too audacious!" Anaya frowned at her daughter's boldness.

"She is just friendly with us, Anu, not audacious. Anyway, I hate to see you working so hard, especially late at night. You need some quality sleep else your blood pressure will fall again. Plus, I am sure you know how important sleep is for the normal functioning of our heart!"

"Oh, not again Nishith. A doctor husband makes you feel in a hospital all the time, always bound by rules and regulations," Anaya protested mockingly.

"Anu, it's not about me being a doctor. It's about me caring for my wife. I hate it when I wake up in the middle of the night or at early dawn and do not find you lying beside me," Nishith said looking at Anaya lovingly.

"How do you manage to charm me even now?" she blushed.

"Well, you see, I am a charming man."

"Oh yeah! Okay I will sleep on time at night, only if you promise to be back home within 8 p.m. every day," Anaya said.

"What sort of a deal is that! You know I can have emergency at any time of the day in the hospital. My patients are important for me..." Nishith explained.

"Nish, I hate it when I feel like going out for a walk in the evening with you and I don't have you here. I hate it when I cook delicious dishes and you come home so late that we can't even dine together. I hate it when I go out for drives alone. How I wish you would have taken me for long drives, Nish! So it's not about you being a doctor, it's about your wife missing you. Get it?" Anaya smiled.

"Okay, you nailed it again, my writer wife! I will try my best to be back home early, but my patients...."

"Even the characters of my book pine for me to write their fate every night, Nish. Do you understand that I create their destiny?"

"Yeah, so in order for us to spend more time with each other, my patients and your fictional characters will have to suffer a little, I guess," Nishith grinned.

***

Nishith arrived at the National Heart Research Centre leaving Anaya back with her serpentine thoughts. The thoughts of losing Nishith, thoughts of being responsible for her cousin's fate and thoughts of Olivia's future made Anaya restless. Olivia had gone to the School of Film and Media Studies to give her admission test and Anaya was all alone at home. She cursed her luck as she could see that her happy family could break into pieces soon. She did not want that to happen. But how could she act as if nothing had happened; she could not be carefree towards Varsha. She dug into the locker of her cupboard and took out a bunch of letters. She read them hopelessly, as if waiting for the words of the letters to alter as she read them, as if waiting for the letters to be her illusion as she stared at them. Those few letters were her biggest enemy at that moment, an enemy which had the potential to ruin her. She whimsically thought of burning those letters, but changed her mind at the last moment. It was the truth of her life and she had to face it. These hidden letters could no more be kept hidden; the truth of the letters had to be revealed. She decided to complete her story in the next couple of days and hand it over to Nishith.

She decided that she'd leave the house after handing Nishith those letters, for she would know not how to face him thereafter. Anaya decided to forward her story to Olivia too so that her daughter could know the truth. Anaya loitered around Olivia's room and her bedroom with a heavy heart. Her heart sank as she saw the family photographs hung on the wall of their living room, and the awards that she, Nishith and Olivia had won over the last few years. They had a perfect family, which she knew was now going to break. What was worse was that neither Nishith nor Olivia has the slightest hint of it. Anaya sobbed at her thoughts and fell asleep on the couch with moist eyes.

SEARCH FOR THE KEY

The doorbell woke her up. It was Zeeshan, a very close friend of Anaya and a fellow writer almost ten years younger to her. Born to an Indian married to a Chinese woman, Zeeshan was fair, quite tall, flaunted the dimple on his right cheek and little brown eyes.

Five years back, Anaya had received a mail from Zeeshan introducing himself as her biggest fan alive on the planet and that he wanted to meet her. Anaya refused to meet him politely, but he was persistent. He wrote a couple of mails saying how much Anaya inspired him to become a writer and to believe in love and be positive in life. In the last mail, Zeeshan attached the manuscript of a novel authored by him and pleaded Anaya to read it once. Anaya was busy penning her own book, but one lazy afternoon, she thought of going through the Word document sent by her biggest fan. The manuscript was a love story between an Indian man and a Chinese woman, which Anaya discovered later was the story of Zeeshan's parents. Anaya was thoroughly impressed by what she read and asked Zeeshan to meet her at the publishing office the next day. She was very impressed with his enthusiasm and understanding of events in a special way. So much so that not only did Anaya and Zeeshan become good friends, they also decided to co-author an anthology of short non-fiction incidents.

"Hey Anaya, I hope I didn't disturb you," Zeeshan bit his lower lip when he saw Anaya rubbing her eyes after opening the door. "Nah! Stop being so formal. I am just sleep-deprived, that's all," Anaya said stifling a yawn.

"All good? You have dark circles beneath your eyes," Zeeshan said as he sat on the couch.

"I told you I am sleep-starved, was working on my new book last night," Anaya said as she sat opposite Zeeshan.

"That's strange! Working on a new book should make you look enthusiastic. But just look at you! You seem to be so lost and distressed. I hope everything is alright," Zeeshan seemed genuinely concerned.

"It's a long story Zee. I don't know where to start from and moreover it will bore you to the bone. Anyway, let's talk about work," Anaya said while tying her hair up in a bun.

"I love long stories, especially when narrated by you. I have all the time," Zeeshan shrugged.

"You won't give up…right?"

"No way! When have I in the past years? Giving up is not listed in my dictionary."

"Yeah, I am well aware of that. Okay let's sit in the balcony. It's a long story, so it'll be better if I get you some tea to keep you engaged," Anaya laughed.

"As you wish, madam."

Anaya told Zeeshan in a nutshell the sequence of events right from the day she had met Nishith for the first time, the way she got married to Nishith, to the current scenario where she could picturise her happy family breaking down. All because of the turn of events, because of her implacable mistake in the past, and because of destiny. She also showed Zeeshan the bunch of letters which she knew were responsible for her current fate. After so many years, Anaya shared her deepest secret with someone on this planet. Though she had known Zeeshan for a few years only, but somehow she had an abundance of trust on him. She felt relaxed after she opened up to Zeeshan as if the hot lava buried in her heart had finally erupted.

"Oh goodness! This charming smile and these pretty eyes have covered such pain underneath, and for so many years. I always thought of you as a woman who had seen a perfect life since birth. Seeing you and Nishith sir, I could never have imagined that you had to struggle so much to earn his love. The respect I had for you has increased manifold, Anaya," Zeeshan said thoughtfully looking at a silent Anaya. It was almost 7 p.m. and neither Zeeshan nor Anaya realize the passage of time.

"Stop praising me! Don't you notice the mistakes I have committed, Zeeshan? I am a horrible woman," Anaya said, looking away from him.

"No Anaya, you are not. Whatever you did was because you loved Nishith sir with all your heart. Your love deserves respect, and nothing else."

"You are blinded by your admiration for my work." After some thought, she said, "Can you do me a favour?"

"You don't have to ask me; just say it and it will be done," Zeeshan said.

"Do you know anyone in Kolkata? I know Nishith's family is rooted there quite influentially, but I cannot ask them now," Anaya asked.

"Oh yes, I have a paternal uncle there. Why what happened?"

"Can you get me any information on the best hospitals or nursing homes for dementia in Kolkata? I have been looking out on the Internet as well, but a personal opinion is always worthier than that," she sighed.

"Okay, I will ask my uncle and give you all the details as soon as possible. What are you planning next, if I may ask?" Zeeshan asked with knotted eyebrows.

"I will leave Singapore within a couple of days and will go to Kolkata to take care of Varsha. I want to provide her with the best treatment and I also want to search for the reason for her isolation. Last I remember, she had been married. Now I really don't know what her in-laws did with her, but I have to find out. Is it possible to track down a few contact numbers with name and address details?" Anaya's hopeful look made Zeeshan's heart melt.

"In India? Well, I will try to find out, but can't guarantee anything on this one."

"I want to have Varsha's husband's contact number. I have very limited information of him, only name, a brief address and the company where he worked. I am restless to know how Varsha landed herself up in the mental hospital. She had no link with Kolkata as far as I remember. Her house was in Mumbai, her in-laws stayed in Pune. Even if she had a memory loss, it is impossible for her to have travelled to Kolkata on her own," Anaya said thoughtfully.

"Things seem way too complicated to me too, Anaya, but you really don't need to leave Singapore, your own house and your family. I am sure Nishith sir will understand once you tell him the truth. He will know that it's not your fault. I am sure," Zeeshan said confidently.

"Zee, Nishith loved Varsha and if Nishith discovers the truth, he will never forgive me," Anaya said almost mechanically, lost in her own thoughts of the consequences of what she had done in the past and what she was going to do in the days to come.

"I agree Nishith sir loved Varsha. But now, you are his love, his family and everything. It is you who matters to him today, Anaya, much more than Varsha. Trust me!"

"Time will now tell who Nishith values more. Right now, I have to worry about my cousin. Her condition would get worse without proper treatment. I just can't bear to see that happen while I live here in perfect bliss. Can you please get me the information, Zee? It will be very helpful to me," Anaya said.

"As soon as possible. And listen, please feel free to call me whenever you seek any help. If you want, I can go to India with you," Zeeshan suggested.

"Thanks a lot for being such a wonderful friend, Zee. I am feeling somewhat free after sharing my burden with you," Anaya said with a smile.

"I am your biggest fan and your true friend. Anything for you, Anaya. But one thing I must say is that you are a very strong woman. The Almighty will help you make a bridge out of all the rough stones that He has kept in your way. Everything will be alright."

"Hope so," Anaya said and Zeeshan half-embraced her before leaving. As Zeeshan opened the door to leave, he saw Nishith standing outside with a cheerful smile.

"Hello Nishith sir," Zeeshan greeted.

"Hey Zeeshan, what's going on?" Nishith asked as he entered the house.

"Just came to discuss about a few incidents for our latest book. It's great to meet you after a long time sir. Hope you are well."

"All the best to you for the book! And I am extremely good, especially because my wife has ordered me to come home before 8 p.m. everyday so that I can take her out for dates and long drives and dinners," Nishith said smiling at Anaya.

"Wow, that's lovely. So you people carry on; I must leave now," Zeeshan said and left.

Nishith looked at Anaya and she looked haggard, "You ordered me to come home by eight and look at yourself! You are not even ready." "I didn't know you took my words so seriously, Nish," Anaya smiled to herself.

"You know what, I would have killed Zeeshan if he would have stayed here longer than five minutes. I have made some great arrangements for my wife and no way was I going to spoil it because of him."

"Thank God Zeeshan left. By the way, you are a doctor, and you are supposed to save people's lives. Words like 'killing' don't suit you at all," Anaya said playfully.

"I feel a little jealous sometimes, since you spend so much time with him. Heart of a man, you won't understand," he winked.

"Then I should also feel jealous of Doctor Radhika…shouldn't I? She spends the entire day in the hospital with you," Anaya said raising her eyebrows.

"Come on, Anu! Doctor Radhika is married. But this man, Zeeshan – one, he is unmarried; two, he adores you, albeit as an author who inspires him. Tell him to settle down; he has crossed thirty-five. I was the father of an eight-year-old daughter at that age," Nishith clarified.

"Okay, I will tell him today itself. Now, will you tell me about the great arrangements you have made for me today? I feel so lucky that my super busy husband has made time for me. I can't even remember the last time we spent some time outside home."

"Stop being sarcastic and get ready! And listen, this is a small present for you. Wear it now," Nishith handed over a big gift box to Anaya.

"What is this?"

"Go inside and see. And please don't take more than half an hour. I am waiting."

GOOD TIMES

Anaya went inside the bedroom and opened the gift box. The black designer sari with red and silver stones all over and the marvellous black pearl set kept on top of it made Anaya scream like a child from her room.

"Nish, I love it. You are the best," Anaya screamed loudly from the bedroom to make her voice reach Nishith.

"Waiting to see you, honey! Make it fast. Oh, don't miss the note inside," Nishith shouted back.

Anaya hurried back to the gift box and after turning it over, got a note written on a red satin paper with golden ink. She read the words with a peaceful and cheerful smile.

Happy anniversary darling! I want to love you for the next hundred years or maybe longer than that. God bless us forever.!

Anaya was astounded by Nishith's gift and wish. The past few days were so tough for her that Anaya had almost forgotten that the next day was their anniversary. Then it struck her that this could be their last anniversary together. She swallowed the lump in her throat and cleared off the tears filling up her eyes.

"Anu, are you praising the jewellery and the sari instead of wearing them? Please hurry up," Nishith's voice interrupted the wave of Anaya's heart-sinking thoughts.

"Just coming, Nish." Anaya said wiping her tears. She did not want to spoil these blissful moments with Nish right now, worrying about the future. The black sari accentuated Anaya's curves and flawless fair skin perfectly, and the ethereal black pearl set complimented it just as well. Anaya was struggling with the knot of her backless black blouse when Nishith entered the room. Nishith had his eyes transfixed on the mirror which reflected Anaya and kept smiling.

"What are you looking at and feeling so happy about, Nish? Help me tie the knot," Nishith approached towards Anaya and tied the knot, his eyes still fixed in Anaya's, although in the mirror. While Anaya cherished his soft touch on her back and his naughty smile in the mirror, Nishith bent a little and whispered in Anaya's ears, "Pristine beauty is what you are, Anu! I love you very much."

"Will you love me forever, Nish? Even if I hurt you unintentionally?" Anaya said turning towards him.

He smiled holding her shoulders, "Didn't you read my note?"

Anaya nodded her head and Nishith kissed her on the forehead, and gave her a quick hug. Anaya tried to drown her grief in Nishith's arms, and his rhythmic heartbeats.

"Do you want to spend the eve of our anniversary in our bedroom or outside?" His eyes twinkled, "For me, the former seems better. What say?" Nishith grinned.

"Shut up! Let's go out. I want to see what my super busy doctor hubby has planned," Anaya said breaking the embrace.

Nishith drove his flamboyant black Audi R8 with Anaya on his side, gazing at him lovingly.

"Are you checking me out?" Nishith asked, trying to focus on driving.

"This song reminded me of the day you first took me for a long drive in Singapore." Anaya said and Nishith laughed as he heard the song playing on the sound box then.

"How do you manage to remember such minute details, Anu?" "Because you are the one I thought about then and think about now. How on earth can I forget anything related to you? It was

one of the most special days of my life when you took me out for a long drive for the first time after we got married, after almost five years of our marriage," Anaya said looking at Nishith.

"I was so insensitive towards you in the initial years of our marriage, Anu. It's your love which made our marriage survive, which made our family be the best family and made me a successful, happy contented man. Without you, this life would be a lie." Nishith said with a sigh when Anaya put her fingers on his lips and started singing the verses of the song being played.

Kuch na kaho....kuch bhii na kaho...

Kya kehna hai...kya sunna hai...

Mujhko pata hai...tumko pata hai...

Samay ka ye pal...tham sa gaya hai...

Anaya giggled as she sang those lines and Nishith continued singing the next few lines.

Aur is pal mein...koi nahin hai...

Bas ek mein hu...bas ek tum ho...

Kuch na kaho...kuch bhi na kaho

Anaya rested her head on Nishith's shoulders and said, "You sing really bad, but I still love your voice."

"That's why I sing only for you, my dear."

Nishith halted the car in front of the Marine Bay and the scenic beauty and the romantic ambience of the place enthralled them both. Though they had been there many times, still the Greenfield site surrounded by water and gardens never failed to mesmerise. The couple strolled around the Waterfront Promenade and enjoyed each other's company. They paused at a breeze shelter after strolling around for a few minutes and got themselves two ice-cream cones. They were surrounded by younger couples; some of them looked at Anaya and Nishith with surprised smiles to see a middle-aged couple at the lovers' spot.

"We are spending some romantic moments after so long, Nish," Anaya said.

"Yes, and it feels so great, making the younger couples jealous of us. We are a much better-looking couple that most of the youngsters here...see!" Nishith said, pulling Anaya near him.

"Anu, can I ask you a silly little question?" Nishith said tucking few strands of Anaya's hair that fell on her eyes due to the breeze.

"Silly question, and you? Seems difficult, but alright," Anaya said.

"Have you ever doubted my love for you?"

"What sort of a question is that?" Anaya was taken aback with this question. "It's not only silly but totally irrelevant."

"I told you it's silly, but you have to answer me. For the initial years of our marriage and for my past, have you ever doubted my love for you?" Nishith asked with a serious tone.

Anaya looked away from Nishith. "Is that a yes? Okay, whom do you think I love the most in this world?" Nishith shot another question.

"Olivia, of course," Anaya said confidently.

"Of course, I love Oli. But I love Oli's mom a little more than her, and a little more than myself," Nishith said looking at Anaya.

"When did you start loving me so much, Nish?" Anaya said, blushing a little.

"As days are passing and I am growing older, I can sense my love for you growing stronger," Nishith held her hand lovingly.

"This is my best anniversary gift, these precious words you uttered just now. I wish I could record these words and hear them again and again," Anaya rested her head on Nishith's shoulders.

That day, they talked about everything: from college days to the present day, their daughter, their love, their marriage and all else. But Nishith, to Anaya's surprise, did not take Varsha's name even once. Anaya could really feel the depth of Nishith's love for her, the depth she had never understood all these days. Nishith and Anaya were totally engrossed in each other's company and the lovely ambience when Olivia's call on Anaya's phone interrupted them.

"Hi, Oli! What happened?"

"Mom, mom I fell from the stairs....there is so much blood. It's paining and I cannot move. Come home soon, please," Olivia said, crying.

"What! How did you fall? Stay right there and don't try to move, okay? Your Dad and I will be home soon, baby," Anaya said and started shivering. "Oli, are you hurt anywhere else? Do you want to call someone from the neighbourhood immediately?"

"No mom, I have just bruised my knees real bad. I am fine. Please ask Dad to drive carefully; I am waiting."

"Nish, we have to rush home. Oli fell from the stairs," Anaya said with trembling lips and ran towards the car.

"What?" Nishith was equally shocked and the frazzled parents hurried towards home.

HAPPY ANNIVERSARY

Anaya and Nishith climbed up the stairs to their flat hurriedly and found the door unlocked. Anaya pushed open the door calling out to Olivia; the dark inside the house terrified her to the bone.

"Oli....Oli...Nishith, why is it so dark inside?" Anaya said grasping Nishith's hands and walking slowly. Then, all of a sudden, the room shone bright with lights and a crowd of almost thirty people greeted them with cheers and applause.

"Happy Anniversary!" The crowd applauded and Anaya spotted Olivia wearing a beautiful red dress, in the pinkest of health, smiling merrily at her parents.

"Is this a way to plan a surprise, Oli? I almost died," Anaya said approaching Olivia.

"I am sorry, mom. I thought that was the only way to get you home quickly. Oh, and dad knew all of it anyway," Olivia said, putting the blame on Nishith. Anaya's mouth fell open at the way Nishith had acted. Nishith bit his lower lip as the truth came out in front of his wife.

"Oh goodness! You knew Olivia was joking? I almost got a mini heart attack there and you must have been laughing inside your head," Anaya said making an annoying face towards Nishith.

"Anu, don't be hysterical. Oli planned this midnight anniversary party for us and wanted my help. You know I can't say no to her," Nishith whispered to Anaya, smiling at the guests.

"I am being hysterical now…am I? I am her mother, Nishith and it kills me to think that something would have happened to her. It is not funny. So you two enjoy the joke and the party, because I am not interested," Anaya was loud when she said this to Olivia and Nishith before entering her bedroom.

The guests – including the fellow doctors working with Nishith, Zeeshan, Anaya's and Olivia's friends – looked at the father and daughter, as if for a hint of what they should be doing now.

"Friends, umm...give me a minute. Anu seems too tired. Just give her a few minutes to freshen up. Till then, you people enjoy the party," Nishith said to the guests and walked inside their bedroom to ebb down his wife's anger. Olivia was totally perplexed due to the course of events and felt guilty about involving her father in her surprise plan. She quickly followed Nishith to soothe her mother down.

"Anu, shall I tell the guests to go home?" Nishith said looking at Anaya who looked away from him.

"Do whatever your daughter says. She has organized this party, after all," Anaya said taking out her pearl ear-rings from her ear.

"She has organized this party for us, Anu, for her parents. I agree she shouldn't have lied about getting hurt, but she is just a child, our baby. Don't spoil her surprise party; she just wanted to make it special for us. If anyone is at fault, it is me," Nishith explained slowly.

"Mom, I am so sorry. I didn't know you will be so hurt and worried. It's seriously not Dad's fault; it was my idea," Olivia hugged Anaya from behind and made a cute puppy face. Anaya turned around, still looking angry at both of them, Wonderful First you plan this up and end up spoiling my mood, and then you compete to take the blame and apologise!" Just when Nishith and Oli exchanged nervous glances, Anaya broke into a laughter. Now, Oli and Nishith exchanged confused glances.

"You think only you two can act," and Anaya continued laughing.

Oli went on to hug both of them and ran out to the living room after a quick, "I am sorry Mom. I will take care of it in future and I love you two."

"So...all this was a good way to teach your madly-in-love husband a lesson," Nishith hugged her. "Our little Oli has become such a big girl," Nishith said to Anaya and picked up the pearl ear-rings which she had taken off. He gently put the ear rings back and offered his arm to her to enter the living room again.

"It is impossible for me to be annoyed with you Nish," Anaya said as Nishith pinned the other ear-ring.

Nishith laughed in response and arm in arm, the couple moved towards the living room to enjoy their twenty-third anniversary party organized by their loving daughter.

"Hey Nishith, Congratulations! Anaya, I must say you look beautiful today," Dr. Radhika said. Anaya knew this good looking doctor was extremely fond of Nishith ever since she had joined the National Heart Centre ten years back. She was totally bewitched by Nishith's intelligence, his nature, and especially the way he loved his wife and daughter.

"My wife always looks beautiful. In fact, I start looking good standing next to her, she has such an aura," Nishith told Dr. Radhika even before Anaya could say something.

"You are so lucky Anaya that Nishith loves you so much," Dr. Radhika said looking at the couple.

"That I am," Anaya said, beaming.

"Special attention, ladies and gentleman!" Oli clapped from the centre of the room. "This is a great day for my Mom and Dad, and of course for me too. In today's times, if I believe in love, it's only because of my Mom and Dad. The bond of love that my parents share cannot be described in words. But you can sure catch a glimpse of it in the smile on Mom's face when she cooks for Dad, and the love dancing in my Dad's eyes every single time he looks at Mom. You are the best couple I have ever seen, even a lot better than my favourite Edward and Bella from the Twilight series." Oli giggled as Anaya rolled her eyes lovingly. "Mom, Dad, please stay in love, forever. For me, the definition of true love is what I see between you two. Cheers to my favourite couple!" Everyone cheered, when Oli cut in with her sweet voice once again, "And here is a small AV of their best moments." Olivia's speech exhilarated both Nishith and Anaya and also the rest of the guests present there.

The AV began showing clippings of Anaya and Nishith that Olivia recorded in her handy cam during several occasions and some of the clippings were recorded beyond Nishith and Anaya's knowledge, especially the morning tea conversation on that day itself when Anaya chided Olivia for listening to her parents' conversation from the corner of the room. The guests applauded and praised the cute moments that their daughter had managed to capture. Anaya rested her head on Nishith's shoulders, enchanted.

She watched the AV with contented eyes while Nishith whispered to Anaya how Olivia had managed to plan such a lovely gift for them. As the AV ended, all the guests clapped and congratulated the couple for holding such a successful and happy marriage.

"Anaya, please do write a story on your married life. Your fans will love to read it," the fellow writer friends said after watching the AV.

"Yes, I am currently working on it," Anaya said looking at Zeeshan who had been quiet throughout, knowing well of the storm that Anaya was struggling through.

"Oh really? You did not even tell me," Nishith said.

"I was planning it as a surprise, Nish." Anaya said patting Nishith's

shoulders and indicating Zeeshan to be normal through her eyes.

"Mom, Dad…come to the dance floor. What are you guys doing here?" Olivia said pulling her parents towards the centre of the room.

"Oli, wait a minute," Anaya said.

"No mom...no more waiting. We have special songs of '90s Bollywood for you to swing on."

Anaya was blushing as Nishith put his arms around her. The music already playing suddenly stopped as Oli changed the song. What played took Anaya and Nishith back to where it had all started.

Mere rang me rangne wali.... Maine Pyar Kiya.

Now was the time when the song really suited them; they were in love. The lights were dimmed, and as they lost themselves in each other's eyes, all the couples joined them.

Nishith looked just as young as ever to Anaya. The memory of the first day when Anaya had seen Nishith, came back to her and she smiled with ecstasy when Nishith held her waist and locked his eyes with hers. Only Anaya could see Nishith as a young man of twenty-one at that time and only Nishith's eyes could see Anaya as a pretty damsel of twenty years despite the fact that they were forty-five years old then. It seemed that they had just fallen in love with each other, again.

"I wish I could meet you again for the first time Anu," Nishith whispered.

"Me too, Nish," Anaya hugged Nishith and matched his footsteps slowly.

"Anu, why is this Rishi hugging Oli?" Nishith said with a changed tone. Anaya turned back and looked at Olivia who was busy dancing with Rishi. "Nishith, they are only dancing. Rishi is Oli's best friend, that's why. Stop being such a possessive Dad," Anaya patted Nishith's arm.

"Hmm."

Anaya turned Nishith's back towards Olivia so that he could no longer see Rishi and Olivia dancing closely.

Nishith and Anaya were so lost in each other that they couldn't comprehend the passage of time. The guests left soon one by one, congratulating the couple once again over the success of their marriage.

"Oli, my baby…Thanks for this lovely surprise. I am so

happy," Anaya said pinching Olivia's cheeks after the guests left.

"Especially the AV. We loved it darling," Nishith said, hugging Olivia.

"I am so happy that you both loved my surprise," Olivia said, grinning from ear to ear.

As both of them moved forward to give Oli a peck, she shouted, much to their horror, "Wait!"

She saw their faces and said, "Oh, wait, let me click a picture in this pose."

Olivia took out her cell phone to click a picture in that pose - her parents planting a peck on one cheek each.

"Your daughter is mad," Anaya commented on Olivia's whimsical attitude.

"Your daughter too!" Nishith winked.

NIGHTMARE

Anaya watched Nishith's dejected and angry face as she entered the bedroom. The pile of letters were all spread over the bed and one of the letters was in Nishith's hand. He was reading it; angst, anger and agony all combined to form a terrible expression on his face. Anaya's heart stopped beating for a minute as she saw that dreadful sight. She remembered vividly that she had forgotten to lock the letters back after showing them to Zeeshan. An invisible rope seemed to entwine Anaya's neck, choking her to death. Anaya came towards Nishith and touched his back gently with her trembling hands. Nishith turned towards her with an unbelievable expression on his face. He did not utter a single word but that look talked tons about what he meant to say to Anaya. She could read hundreds of questions on Nishith's face, questions for which Anaya did not have any answers. Anaya cupped Nishith's face with her hands and tried to speak with trembling lips, but Nishith abdicated her touch on his skin. Nishith merely dug out a small briefcase from the cupboard, threw in a few essentials in it and rushed out of the house. Before entering his car, he looked up at Anaya standing in the balcony, teary-eyed, and shook his head, as if to say, "I could never imagine you could do such a thing with me...with Varsha."

Anaya shouted and screamed out Nishith's name with tears pouring down her eyes constantly, but Nishith did not pay any heed to her tears, or her screams. He just drove away.

"Nishith!" Anaya sprang from the bed with tears running down her eyes and breathing heavily.

"What happened, Anu?" Nishith woke up, hearing Anaya's scream and switched on the bed-side lamps.

She embraced him and cried, realising within a few seconds that it was a cursed dream, a dream that had seemed so unbelievably realistic to her. She could not forget the look on Nishith's face and the way he had left her. Her tears became more profuse and her breaths got heavier. Nishith hugged her tightly as he saw Anaya in that miserable condition. Never in his life had he seen Anaya in such a tattered state; he always knew Anaya to be stronger than him.

"Anu, relax. I am with you, dear. What happened? Why are you crying so badly?" Nishith said wiping Anaya's tears and taking Anaya's head closer to his chest.

"Nish…I can't live without you and Oli," Anaya managed to utter amidst sobs.

"Can we survive without you, Anu? We love you so much. You are our life-system," Nishith assured, kissing Anaya on her forehead.

Anaya nodded her head and hugged Nishith firmly.

"Here, have some water! You are still breathing so heavily," Nishith poured a glass of water from the jug without breaking the embrace.

Anaya drank the water and calmed down.

"It was just a dream, Anu. What did you see to have terrified you so much?" Nishith said running his finger through Anaya's hair.

"It was a cursed dream, worse than any nightmare," Anaya said softly.

"What did you see? Tell me and you will feel better." Nishith insisted. "I saw you left me, and this house," Anaya said with a lump in her throat.

"I can never leave my life, Anu. It was a dream due to some people's jealousy of seeing us happy together. Got it? Such dreams never come true," Nishith said caressing Anaya's right cheek lovingly.

"You are right, Nish," Anaya smiled.

"Now try to sleep; you will wake up fresh and happy," Nishith said and made Anaya lie down on the bed and covered her till her shoulders with the blanket.

Anaya kept gazing at Nishith with content eyes as he played the role of the world's best husband.

"Do you want to tell me something, Anu?" Nishith sounded worried. "Is there anything that is troubling you, except this dream?" Nishith asked.

"Not at all," Anaya lied and thought if only she could share the sea of secrets locked in her heart with Nishith.

"Go to sleep, Anu," Nishith said and Anaya closed her eyes. Nishith fell asleep soon, but Anaya couldn't let sleep catch her eyes. She kept tossing in bed as she thought about the dream. The more she tried to forget the dream, the more it became vivid to her eyes. Finally, after trying for half an hour, she sat on the bed and kept staring at Nishith sleeping. Only a couple of days and she knew she'd have to leave this house. She kept gazing at Nishith with a heavy heart, thinking of days ahead of her, that she would have to survive without Nishith. She did not know whether he would forgive her and if their separation would be a temporary or a permanent one. She wanted to wake him up and embrace him, till fate separated them. She was looking at Nishith, her emotions raging inside her heart, when a drop of tear escaped her eyes and fell on Nishith's cheek.

"You're still awake, Anu!" Nishith half opened his eyes as her "It's almost 5 am and I can't sleep," Anaya said looking away from Nishith, in order to hide her tears.

"Okay," he got up and looked at her. "Let's talk."

"No, Nish. You please sleep; I will read something. We slept at 3 and you have slept merely two hours."

"Oh, come on. Let's sit in the balcony and talk over a cup of tea. I can't sleep if my wife is feeling so restless. Moreover, I want to talk to you, Anu," Nishith said and insisted that she makes them both tea.

Anaya and Nishith sat in the balcony with their morning tea and looked at the calm sky, the breaking of the night into dawn, and drowned themselves in the freshness of the morning breeze touching their skin.

"You know Anu, there is a seventeen-year-old kid admitted in our hospital who is suffering from rheumatic heart disease. Her heart valves are infected and tomorrow I have to operate on her. There are very little chances of her survival, though I am going to try my level best. She is almost of our Olivia's age; I feel miserable whenever I talk to her parents. They have kept all their hope on me, they are treating me like God and I know there is little chance of making that little girl, Pooja survive. If I can't save her, I will feel so defeated, Anu."

"You will save her, Nish. Don't be pessimistic. Even if there are very little chances of her survival, you will give her moments to live and cherish each moment. God can't be so hostile towards such a kid," Anaya said patting Nishith's shoulders.

"Her valves have to be replaced tomorrow. Moreover, the inner tissues of her heart are also infected. It is a major operation and this girl suffers from anaemia. Only by God's grace, I want to save her, Anu. She is completely like our Oli, so full of life. If I can't save her..." Nishith was about to continue when Anaya put her finger on his lips. teardrop fell on his cheek.

"Sshh! You will save her. I will pray to God, and He will make you save her. Have faith in yourself. You see Oli in her, right? Just think while operating that you are on a mission to save your own daughter. No negative power on this earth can stop you from saving her. Trust me," Anaya assured Nishith.

"You are right, Anu. I feel so good and confident after sharing this with you," Nishith said holding Anaya's hands.

"Can I come with you to the hospital? I want to meet Pooja and her parents. I want to assure them that she is in safe hands," Anaya said sipping the remnants of her tea.

"Really? Do you have that much faith in me?" Nishith said with a new hope flickering on his face.

"Yes, I am confident. My husband is the best doctor of this world." Anaya replied with a smile.

LIFE AND DEATH

Anaya went to the National Heart Centre with Nishith to visit Pooja. The very sight of the little girl who was sleeping under the heavy effect of antibiotics at the ICU terrified Anaya. Pooja has been kept through mechanical ventilation to assist her breathing. There were intravenous lines for drug infusion through a channel done on her right wrist.

"Her mitral valve has become laden with calcium which has totally disrupted the normal functioning of the valve. I have been treating her with antibiotics since two weeks but there is no improvement. Her valve seems to have undergone chronic damage. The only option left with me is surgery and I have to replace her valve before some permanent heart muscle damage occurs," Nishith explained to Anaya as she looked at him.

"What are the chances of her survival? Do her parents know about the situation?" Anaya said after a sigh.

"Since she suffers from anaemia, there are less chances of a successful operation. I wish she doesn't go into a coma," Nishith said thoughtfully.

"Good Morning, Anaya. Good Morning, Dr. Nishith," Dr. Radhika said approaching them.

"Morning, doctor. What is her current condition?" Nishith asked. "Not good. I will suggest you operate today itself. Her heartbeats are sinking. Haemoglobin level shows no improvement and just have a look at the ECG report..." Dr. Radhika handed Nishith the report over and Anaya looked at Nishith with tensed eyes.

Nishith nodded his head distressfully as he read the reports.

"So what's your take on it?" Dr. Radhika asked.

"I have to talk to her parents. They have to sign the papers. As soon as I get their consent, I will operate," Nishith said handing the reports back to Dr. Radhika.

"Good! Let me prepare the papers," Dr. Radhika said and left towards the entrance of the hospital.

"Are you okay?" Anaya said softly, perplexed by the course of events.

"I feel stressed," Nishith uttered.

"It is not the first time that you are operating such a critical patient. Be confident and be yourself," Anaya said with a beam of hope in her eyes.

"Can you accompany me in talking to Pooja's parents?" Nishith asked.

Anaya nodded and walked with him. The sight of her parents' fear-laden faces and their hope towards Nishith scared Anaya; she could sense the pressure Nishith must be under. Nishith patiently explained to them about the bond they had to sign to give their consent for such a major operation. The parents had already been upset, and this scared them further. Pooja's mother couldn't control her tears and begged Nishith to save her daughter's life.

"Doctor, we don't have anyone except her in our life. Please save her, else we will die along with her." Pooja's mother folded her hands and pleaded to Nishith while Nishith tried his best to be emotionally neutral.

"Have faith in God and everything will be alright. My husband will give the best of his life to save your daughter," Anaya said hugging the poor mother.

"Are you that famous writer?" Pooja's mother uttered slowly between her tears. Anaya nodded her head looking at Nishith.

"My daughter wanted to be like you. She has read all your books. You know, oh God! She wanted to meet you...If only I knew..." Pooja's mother said wiping her tears.

"I will meet her before the operation," Anaya said and looked at Nishith who nodded his head in response.

Nishith gave Anaya the hospital robe to wear before entering the ICU. Anaya and Nishith went near Pooja's bed and Nishith touched her forehead gently, which made Pooja open her eyes with difficulty. She was having problem in breathing and the very sight made Anaya break into tears. Nishith signalled to Anaya to be emotionally stable and talked to Pooja.

"Hi Pooja! Just look who has come to meet you. Your favourite author, Anaya Chatterjee," Nishith said and smiled.

"Hi Pooja. Your mother said you have read all of my books and that you want to be a writer too," Anaya said smiling towards Pooja who smiled back in response, recognizing her.

"Ma'am, you are my idol," Pooja spoke with great difficulty.

"Don't talk, Pooja. Today, you have a small operation. Once you are fine, you can come home and chat endlessly with your favourite author," Nishith said calmly, but all colour vanished from Pooja's face out of fear.

"Don't be scared. Everything will be alright. It's just a small operation after which you will feel much better," Anaya said with much difficulty as she tried to check her emotions. Anaya walked out of the ICU and broke down.

"Are you okay?" Nishith said after coming out a few minutes later.

"I pray you save that girl's life. May all of the world's good luck and prayers be with you for today's operation," Anaya said.

"Thanks, Anu. You should go home now. I will be busy with the arrangements of the operation," Nishith said patting Anaya's shoulders.

Anaya returned home with a heavy heart and prayed to God to save Pooja's life; the girl had her whole life ahead of her. She could not put her concentration anywhere else until she got Zeeshan's call.

"Anaya, I have traced the numbers of Varsha's father and her husband. I am texting you those numbers. Hope it comes to your use," Zeeshan said in one breath.

"Thanks a ton, Zee. You don't know what you have done for me," Anaya said and disconnected the phone.

Anaya was trapped in a quandary about who she should call first. After thinking for about a minute, she dialled her uncle's number, holding her breath.

"Hello?" A coarse voice of an old man could be heard on the

other side of the phone. Anaya immediately recognized it.

"Can I talk to Varsha?" Anaya asked without revealing her identity.

"Varsha....who are you?" The old man's voice was lined by surprise and shock hearing Varsha's name.

"I am a friend. Can you give me her contact number?" Anaya said.

There was an awkward silence after which the old man's voice broke into tears.

"Uncle, why are you crying?" Anaya said with exasperation.

"Varsha is missing since three years. We have given lots of advertisements in newspapers and news channels, but haven't got clue of her. May be she is dead..." The old man's voice got choked and he disconnected the call leaving Anaya speechless.

A living person is considered dead to her own parents. How unfair! Anaya collected herself and dialled Varsha's husband.

"Who is it?" An angry, stern male voice spoke on the other end of the phone.

"Can I talk to Varsha?" Anaya repeated the same set of words.

"I don't know anyone by this name. Wrong number," the male voice spoke firmly.

"Don't lie! She is your wife," Anaya said with anger.

"She was my wife. Now I have married Ronita," the male voice shouted.

"You bastard! What have you done with Varsha that she is missing since years?" Anaya yelled.

"What have I done? Nothing! She was a mad woman, unable to remember anything. I threw her out of my house in anger and I don't know where she is, and don't even wish to know," the man explained with a roughness in his tone.

"Instead of taking her to the doctor and taking care, you threw her out of the house? Men like you should be burnt alive," Anaya shouted.

"First you tell me who the hell are you to tell me all this after so many years? And if you were so concerned, where were you all this while?" The silence between them was heart-wrenching, when the man suddenly spoke up in a voice more deadly than the deathly silence, "Varsha is dead...If she were still alive, there would have been some trace of her. So stop lecturing me about a dead person and mind your own business." He hung up.

Anaya could not believe the fate of her cousin sister. Varsha was not an orphan like her, she had her parents to care for her, and she had gotten married to a rich businessman. And today, she is rotting in a mental asylum without treatment. The whole world including Varsha's parents think her to be dead.

Anaya splashed water on her face and when she looked up in the mirror, she saw Varsha's face. She was the only one who knew how Varsha was and her whereabouts. The doorbell woke her from her reverie. She hurriedly wiped her face dry and opened the door. Nishith stood there, bathed in sweat, tears and a few specks of blood on his shirt. Nishith entered the house without any words and sat on the sofa. Anaya was scared to see him thus.

"Here, have some water," Anaya handed him a glass which he drank without any word or gestures.

"Are you okay?" Anaya said, gently touching Nishith's shoulder.

Nishith hugged her like a scared little child as tears bathed his cheeks.

"I couldn't save Pooja. She is dead Anaya. I couldn't save that little girl...I could not save her from the heart failure," Nishith cried his heart out.

"It's not your fault, Nishith. Maybe she had but these few years to live on this earth," Anaya said consoling her husband.

"She deserved to live, Anu. And I couldn't save her." Nishith descended on the floor from the sofa as his tears became heavier. Anaya hugged Nishith and cried with him. Tears for a seventeen-year-old girl who had idolised Anaya, tears for Varsha who was dead to the world but alive in her as her guilt, and tears for herself and Nishith...for they were to separate soon. All her agony weighing on her, an enormous volcano of tears erupted from Anaya's eyes. She embraced Nishith and the couple kept crying for very long, sitting on the floor.

A NEW DAWN

Life doesn't stop for anyone and humans have no control over death. Death is like a beautiful woman who always walks by our side, waiting to hug us. Neither can we see this woman, nor does she listen to our pleadings ever. She is governed by her own wills and whims. We have to live with the mortals, just like mortals, and overcome the grief of death of our loved ones until death hugs us too, silently one day.

"Morning! Here's your coffee," Anaya handed Nishith his coffee mug as he browsed through the newspaper headlines absent-mindedly.

"I don't feel like going to the hospital today," Nishith said after a sigh.

"You are a doctor, Nishith. Dealing with life and death is religion part of your work. If you couldn't save one life does not imply that you will lock yourself inside your house. You have other patients waiting for treatment. They need you now," Anaya said clutching Nishith's hand. She could see he had been upset all along. Seeing Oli in Pooja hadn't really helped him in this case.

"I am just taking off for a day Anu," Nishith said looking at Anaya.

"You are not just taking a day off. You are mourning for the life you could not save yesterday. I know that every time such things happen, you feel depressed and blame yourself. Though you never show this side of yours to anyone in the hospital, I know the tornado of thoughts that hit you when something like this occurs," Anaya explained.

"It's not so easy Anu. Life of doctors is hell when they can't save a patient they get attached to."

"I know, but mourning for the inevitable won't change anything. Your patients need you and once you go to the hospital and treat your patients, you will feel better. Trust me."

"On the contrary, whenever I will enter the ICU, Pooja's smiling face will haunt me."

"Do you want to keep your patients untreated? They must be waiting for you."

"Some other doctors will treat them," Nishith said lowering his face.

"You can't be partial with your patients. Once you go through the next surgery successfully, all the bad feeling with yesterday's incident will fade. It is your duty," Anaya said holding Nishith's hands within hers.

"How do you manage to be so practical despite being so emotional?" Nishith asked Anaya.

"Because I am the best," Anaya said and giggled.

"You are! The way you pull me out from such situations is incredible." He hugged her from the chair itself. "I wonder what I would do without you. I would be a horrible doctor, I guess."

"Seriously! Just as I would never have been a writer without you," Anaya said.

"You have an answer for everything…don't you?" Nishith laughed.

"Pros of being a writer, I guess. Now you go, get ready. You are already late," Anaya said, pushing him off his chair.

After Nishith went to the hospital on Anaya's persuasion, Anaya dialled the number of Howrah Mental Hospital to ask about Varsha.

"Can I talk to Mrs. Das?" Anaya asked the male voice who received the call.

"Yes, hold for a minute." The voice said in return and Anaya waited to talk to the nurse she had met that day in Kalighat.

"Hello, who is it?" A shrill, loud female voice asked.

"Hello Mrs. Das. I am Anaya Chatterjee. I met you in Kalighat a few days back. I am Varsha's cousin sister," Anaya said making an effort to remind her.

"Oh yes, Mrs. Chatterjee. How can I help you?" She remembered Anaya.

"How is Varsha?" Anaya asked immediately.

"She is not well. She doesn't eat and sleep properly. Basically, she is living a dead life," Mrs. Das replied in a grave tone.

"Does she talk?" Anaya asked. Her heart was in her mouth and her conscience was gnawing at her.

"Seldom, only when she gets me by her side, and that too when she can remember me. These patients need a lot of love and care from people they are close to. She has not told us of anyone, nor has anyone claimed to remember her. She would have been better dead, than live such a cursed life," Mrs. Das's voice cracked and Anaya could fathom that she was very serious.

"How can you say such a thing? I have but one request from you. I will be in Kolkata within a week's time and I will take her to a place where she can be treated well. I am sure she will recover from her illness," Anaya said with a false confidence, more to gather herself up than Mrs. Das.

"I hope so, but...anyway, I will be waiting for you," Mrs. Das said.

"Please prepare the papers. I will be there within a week. Take care of my sister till then, please," Anaya said earnestly.

"I am glad you are coming back for her, because her conditioning is worsening. Along with people and places in her life, she is now at a stage where she is forgetting to follow her daily routine, like combing her hair, eating, sleeping, and all that comes so naturally. I am sure she will feel better once you take her to a neurologist,"

"I will be there as soon as I can. Thank you so much, Mrs. Das." Anaya thanked the benevolent nurse and disconnected the call.

She drove to Zeeshan's house immediately thereafter.

"Hey Anaya, what a pleasant surprise!" Zeeshan greeted Anaya.

"Listen Zee, I need to gather some information about the best dementia treatment centre in Kolkata. So I will leave Singapore within a week. Here is my pen drive, the short stories for our anthology are all here. Please don't hesitate to go ahead and publish it in my absence, as I won't return here unless Varsha's condition gets better. I will give all the letters to Nishith and I will also mail him my story. I wish he reads it and understands the reason behind hiding such an integral truth from him," Anaya said in one breath.

"So, you are determined to leave Singapore?" Zeeshan asked.

"Yes, I will leave. That will be the best for everyone," Anaya said with a heavy heart.

"What about Olivia? I am sure she is too young to digest such a hard truth. I don't know, at your anniversary party it seemed she idealises you two and your relationship. Have you thought what it could do to her impressionable mind?" Zeeshan said shaking his head.

"Olivia is my life, just like Nishith and she needs to know. I will leave her a note. I know she will hate me after knowing the truth and so will Nishith. But you know, Zee, if my love crosses this hurdle, nothing in the world would be able to beat it. Moreover, I need to get rid of this guilt. And I will pay any cost for it," Anaya's eyes watered.

"Listen, in the little way that I can help, I can go to Kolkata and look after Varsha. You can stay here and take care of things. I will keep you updated about whatever takes place there," Zeeshan offered.

"No way, Zee. First of all, you are a stranger to Varsha and she won't be comfortable. Secondly, why will you leave everything here and go to Kolkata for a stranger?"

"It's not about Varsha; it's for you. I don't want you to stab your own happiness," Zeeshan replied.

"I can't be happy if I hide this truth any further, Zee. I have already locked this truth inside my heart for more than fifteen years. I can't anymore," Anaya said with a sigh.

"But can you live without Nishith Sir and Olivia?" Zeeshan asked her earnestly.

"Don't try to break my resolve, Zee. Please be my strength, since only you know what I am going through right now. Don't make me weak, please."

"Alright, if that's what you want, then I am with you. I will mail you the details of dementia treatment centres as soon as I collect information and you promise me that you will not hesitate to tell me whenever you need any help," Zeeshan said finally with a smile.

She thanked him and returned home. Her thoughts went to Nishith and his pain for Pooja. He returned from the hospital a little later and he seemed to have revived his composure and confidence after the two successful surgeries of that day. Anaya was happy to see Nishith in an improved mental state. After a light dinner, Nishith went to sleep.

Anaya went to the study at midnight and opened the folder named "The hidden letters". She started from where she had left the story. She went twenty years back in time as she sipped her midnight coffee and sat in front of her desktop. She took a deep sigh and started writing again…

A ROSE BUD

It was the first time Anaya was travelling by air. While the flight was taking off, Anaya's lips trembled out of jitteriness. She was not yet comfortable with Nishith because he blamed her for his separation with Varsha. Anaya was so tempted to hold his hand to ward off her fear of flying, but she was scared to do so. Nishith observed Anaya's trembling lips when the flight took off, and somewhere felt guilty that he could not make her feel comfortable.

"Are you alright?" Nishith whispered in Anaya's ears after the flight took off successfully.

"Much better," Anaya said biting her lower lip.

Nishith nodded his head and thoughts of Varsha returned to his mind. Varsha's laughter, her endless talks; Varsha's face hugged his mind as he closed his eyes. How he wished it was Varsha accompanying him to Singapore as his wife. Watching Anaya's face made him remember that he had lost Varsha; and that there was no chance of return. The painful separation with his first love made him hate Anaya. He did not want to inflict Anaya with such pain, but the person who was himself broken couldn't have mended anyone else's heart. His mother had taken a promise from him that he would treat Anaya well in the unknown country and would not make her suffer for a fault that wasn't hers. Nishith knew well that he couldn't be cruel to Anaya, but he didn't know anything about loving her. He could never replace Varsha with Anaya. He could never love Anaya. Since both Anaya and Nishith had been victims of unrequited love, she knew he would be lost in Varsha's thoughts more often than she could point out. His love for Varsha was way too strong. Both of them knew the taste of each other's pain, but were helpless to ebb down each other's suffering. Anaya looked at Nishith from the corner of her eye and wished she could hug him just once, and rest her head on his chest. It had been two years since they were married and except sharing this name of a relationship, they shared nothing. They hardly had anything to talk to each other about. Anaya took a sigh and prayed to God to make things better between them.

As the flight was about to land, Anaya closed her eyes with trembling lips, chanting a prayer. Nishith put his hand over hers and pressed it slightly. Anaya looked at Nishith and he gave her a look of assurance. Did my prayer start working already?

Nishith's uncle received Anaya and Nishith at the Singapore airport.

"My boy, Nishith, you are a lucky man! Such a good-looking wife... Hello Anaya. I am Nishith's favourite uncle," he smiled at both of them.

"Hello Uncle," Anaya touched his feet and he looked elated. "I have heard a lot about you from mom and dad. It's a pleasure meeting you." Anaya said cheerfully. Doctor Uncle had a charming demeanour with a happy-go-lucky face. He was a man in his fifties, short in height, wore a white hat matching with his white suit in order to protect him from the scorching sun of Singapore. Anaya instantly liked his company.

"Did you have a good flight?" He asked courteously, and she could see traces of a smile on Nishith's lips.

"It was okay. My first time."

He laughed and asked both of them, "So, love marriage, eh?" "Yes." Anaya said. "No," Nishith replied at almost the same time.

Uncle smiled with a perplexed look, trying to analyze who lied.

"It was an arranged marriage, uncle. Right, Anaya?" Nishith said.

"Actually yes, but I had fallen in love with Nishith days before our marriage," Anaya replied hesitatingly.

"Wow, this is awesome. What about you Nishith? I am also a fool enough to ask you. Which guy won't fall in love with a girl like Anaya?" Doctor Uncle smiled.

"So we will be living in Clementi…right uncle?" Nishith asked changing the topic.

"Yes, you people must be tired. Let me take you to your new house. Hope you like it," he said giving the keys to Nishith.

The hour-long drive did not seem very long because Uncle was a jovial man. He told them that he had an emergency to rush to, so he would quickly drop them and get in touch soon. Anaya was exhilarated to see their new house. It was a one-floor house with two bed rooms, a drawing-dining room, a kitchen and two attached bathrooms. There was a lawn in front of the house which made it look beautiful. Anaya's face broke into a big smile as she strolled around the house.

"Where does Uncle stay, Nishith?" Anaya asked.

"Tanglin Area," Nishith sat on the couch without any joy or excitement visible on his face on seeing their new house.

"Isn't the house pretty, Nishith? We should give a nice name to it. Suggest a name," Anaya said sitting beside Nishith.

"I don't know. Stop talking about such childish stuff. Every house doesn't need a name; an address is enough," Nishith sounded irritated.

"Yeah, just like every marriage doesn't need love; staying together is enough," Anaya replied, hurt.

"What was the need to tell Uncle that ours was a love marriage?" Nishith shouted.

"I corrected him later, didn't I? It was me who fell in love with you, days before our marriage," Anaya clarified.

"There was no need to tell him such details. One more thing, I want to make it clear to you that I married you because my mother compelled me to do so. She treats you as her daughter and her love for you made me marry you. I love Varsha and will keep loving her, irrespective of what she feels about it. Our marriage is nothing but a compromise from my side. I cannot reciprocate your love Anaya," Nishith said in one breath as Anaya's eyes welled up.

Anaya nodded her head as tears crawled down her beautiful eyes.

"Choose any one bedroom for yourself and I will sleep in the other one. And if you feel I am spoiling your life, you can opt to move on. You are young, beautiful and pretty intelligent. There will be plenty of men who will value you more than me. Goodnight. I have to go to the hospital at 8 a.m. tomorrow," Nishith said and walked towards the bathroom to freshen up.

Anaya's tears made no difference to him. Nishith's indifference killed every bit of happiness she had felt on seeing their new house and reaching a new country. She walked towards a bedroom and called up her mother-in-law.

"Anaya! You reached? How is your new house?" Mrs. Chatterjee yelped in joy hearing Anaya's voice.

Anaya kept crying on the phone like a kid who had been separated from her mother.

"Did Nishith misbehave with you?" Mrs. Chatterjee asked concerned.

"Nishith will never be able to love me, Mom. I am missing you so much and feeling so lonely without you. I don't have anyone in this city, in this big country, even to talk to ," Anaya's tears became heavier.

"Calm down, Anu. You are worrying for no reason. My prayers are always with you dear. Just give a little time to yourself and Nishith. Your marriage is like a rose bud. With time, it will bloom to a beautiful rose. Have faith. You are my strong daughter." Mrs. Chatterjee consoled Anaya.

"Thanks Mom. I love you."

"Now go to sleep. You must be really tired. One good sleep will make you feel much better and will make you regain your composure," Mrs. Chatterjee advised Anaya and disconnected the call.

Anaya lay on the bed but sleep evaded her eyes. She went to the terrace of their new house and watched the new city of Clementi. The stars, the moon and the breeze seemed to whisper something. The solitude around her and the calmness of the night enabled her to feel the hope in this new country.

She knew Nishith did not love her now, but there is no prediction for future. He could fall in love with her; his behaviour could change. When a rose plant bears a bud, no one knows whether the bud will be eaten up by insects or birds, or bloom into a beautiful rose. Anaya felt contented with the hope in her life and looked forward to the next day. She finally slept in the separate bedroom after watching Nishith sleep and blowing him a kiss in the air.

SETTLING DOWN

The next morning, Nishith was surprised to find the living room completely in order. Though they had come to their new house just last night, no one could have guessed that. Nishith checked the next bedroom to find Anaya missing.

He called out Anaya's name but did not get any response. As he was growing a little apprehensive, he saw Anaya entering the house from the main door with two bags.

"Good morning, Nishith! Could you sleep well last night?" Anaya greeted him with a cheerful smile.

"Morning. Where have you been?" Nishith asked a little confused.

"My dearest husband, you have to go to the hospital by 8 a.m. There is no food in the house, so I went to buy some bread, butter, eggs and fruits to prepare breakfast for you." Anaya said as she went to the kitchen to keep the food stuffs.

"There was absolutely no reason to worry so much. We could have eaten in the neighbourhood café," Nishith said with a yawn.

"It's not such an excellent idea to kill our money. Moreover, we are not bachelors; we have to make this house our home. You get it? I guess no. Anyway, you freshen up. Let me prepare breakfast," Anaya said and Nishith stood amazed by her presence of mind.

The doorbell rang and Anaya was delighted to find Doctor Uncle there. He had come to accompany Nishith to the National Heart Centre where Nishith was to work as an intern under him and simultaneously complete his M.D. to become a successful cardiologist.

"Anaya…this house looks so tidied up and decorated. When did you manage to set up your house?" Doctor Uncle asked with delight.

"Uncle, I woke up pretty early in the morning today. This is my own house. How can I not give it all my time?" Anaya beamed. "Join us for breakfast, please."

"Sure dear. Where is Nishith?" Doctor Uncle said with a smile.

"There he is." Anaya pointed to Nishith who entered the living room dressed in a sky blue-white check shirt and jeans. Nishith wore his rimless glasses which gave him the look of a very handsome and reserved doctor. Anaya's heart skipped a beat as she saw Nishith approaching towards the dining table. Nishith's eyes met Anaya's and she took her eyes off him as soon as she could. After having egg sandwiches and a fruit salad for breakfast, Nishith left for the hospital with Uncle.

"Anaya, listen," Nishith said before leaving the house.

"First, you listen! Take the entire world's best wishes and good luck for your first day at the hospital. By what time will you return home?" Anaya asked.

"Thank you. I will be back by 8 p.m. and will call you at regular intervals. You have lunch in time and take care of yourself," Nishith said and left. Anaya nodded her head and smiled at Nishith's concern for her.

After Nishith left home, Anaya unpacked and started arranging her clothes and his in the wardrobe in each room. She also took out and arranged other stuff such as cosmetics, books, accessories, music CDs and kept them in their respective places. It was just around noon and she had arranged their entire house. Anaya took a notebook and made a list of things that they needed, i.e. foods, oil, spices, soap, toothpaste, washing powder and some utensils. Anaya decided to visit the supermarket close to their house and get herself the listed things. She wore a kurti and jeans and went to the shopping complex about fifteen minutes walking distance from her house. After buying the necessary household material, she decided to get herself some new dresses too. Most of the women she saw in this city wore western casual outfits and Anaya did not want to look like a fish out of water by wearing the same old salwar suits. She bought herself four graphic t-shirts, two skirt and a narrow-fit jeans. Since she was not very meaty, all the outfits complimented her nearly perfect figure. She also bought a travel guide of Singapore to know more about the country.

As she was about to return home, she thought of having lunch, for it was already past lunch time. She entered the nearby Chinese restaurant and ordered a plate of gravy vegetable noodles and a salad. She browsed through the travel guide while waiting for her food to come. All this while, she had been thinking that she will be bored to death when Nishith would be at work, but she saw her destination printed in blue ink on the travel guide. A smile of contentment kissed her lips as she saw the National Library close by. She had her lunch with a smile as she knew what she needed to do next. She wanted to go to the library that very moment but with half a dozen bags in her hand, it would have been too odd.

When she reached home, the phone beeped with a missed call. It was Nishith's. She called back on the hospital number and asked for him. When he came on the line a couple of minutes later, his voice sounded concerned.

"Where have you been?" Nishith asked on the other side of the phone.

"I was out for lunch and was shopping," Anaya said.

"You have plunged into it from the first day. You know, you will be here for quite a while. Anyhow, good that you had lunch. Will you stay at home now or you plan to be exploring the city?"

Nishith said and laughed thinking about Anaya's restless nature.

"Actually I was planning to go somewhere," Anaya said smiling.

"Where?" Nishith was curious.

"The National Library. I think I will go have a look and if I like it, will take up membership there so that I can go and read whatever I want. My days will pass well and I will have something productive to do. I hope you understand what I mean."

"Well do you know how to reach there? Are you sure it won't be a problem?" Nishith said in a concerned tone.

"Yes, I have bought a travel guide and there are all details related to reaching this place. And don't worry, I will be back home before you are. By the way, how is your day going in the hospital? Did you have your lunch?" Anaya asked.

"Day is pretty good and I had lunch too. Okay, you take care and call me if there is any problem. Bye," Nishith said.

Anaya smiled to herself; Nishith was concerned about her. There was hope.

She left for the library a little while later and reached without any problem. The instructions in the travel guide were accurate. Upon reaching the library, Anaya felt so lively. She had not felt so good ever since she had left college. She enrolled herself as a member of the library without any delay. She browsed through all the sections of the library and took out a book named Divine red Happiness. She sat in a wooden chair with the book and started reading it. Just then, a man in his thirties sat in the chair opposite hers. He looked a non-Indian, probably European who had golden brown hair and a pink-white complexion. He sat with some French book and looked at Anaya at frequent intervals, popping his eyes from the book. Anaya wondered if she looked odd in the red t-shirt she wore, or was there something else wrong. Diverting her attention from the man opposite her, Anaya read the book. A quote of it instantly instilled in her some positive vibes.

Being yourself is what you call divine happiness. Happiness is sacred only when you respect God's creation that is you. God created you with perfection and by being yourself, you can taste sacred happiness.

She read a bit about people who had messed up their lives in trying to change themselves for the one they loved or the one they had married. People think their entire life that their surroundings and their near ones are the only ones who can make them happy. It is such a myth. By being yourself, by being God's creation, you can be the happiest. Anaya felt sanguine about her life and smiled to herself as she murmured the beautiful quote again. The European looked up as Anaya murmured the quote with a smile; she felt awkward as he caught her speaking something out loud.

"Sorry," Anaya murmured.

"There you go wrong, madam. Just now you were reading that happiness is being yourself, then why are you being sorry for being yourself?" The European asked with a smile and Anaya laughed as she realized.

"You are right," Anaya said.

"Hey, I am Frank. I run the Clementi Primary School."

"Hello, I am Anaya. I came to Singapore just yesterday and am still trying to figure your city out."

"Are you an Indian? Where do you stay in Singapore?"

"Yes, I am from India. I am staying with my husband in Clementi."

"Excellent. Since you stay close by, would you like to come over and see our school? And maybe if things go well and our requirements are fulfilled, you could consider working as a primary teacher in my school?"

"Are you serious? I would love to." Anaya was overjoyed.

"Yes I am. My school needs some teachers and I felt you can be an efficient candidate. Here's my card." Frank gave Anaya his business card.

"You can come for an interview tomorrow or the day after."
"Thank you, Frank. I would come and see you there tomorrow. Tell me the time," Anaya said taking the card.

"How about 10 a.m.?" Anaya nodded and Frank left the library after a customary goodbye.

Wow! This country is really doing some miracle. My wishes are coming true. Anaya shared the news with Nishith who seemed equally happy with Anaya's will to work. He knew it would keep her occupied and not leave space for negative thoughts.

The next day, Anaya went to the Clementi Primary School at the decided time and to her luck and talent, was hired. She thanked Frank and was too excited for her new job where she would be able to spend a lot of time with kids. Anaya's life really had some spark after landing in Singapore. She had a job in the morning at the school, a hobby to nurture in the evening at the library. Life started to love Anaya as she learned to love life. Nishith was happy with his work at the hospital and studied after coming home. Life has started getting busier for both Nishith and Anaya as they managed to settle down well in a new country.

ABERRATION

Anaya and Nishith were still exploring – a new job, a new country, new people – and spent time with each other, though not as lovingly as a husband and wife should. More than two years slipped easily in this fashion and Nishith completed his M.D. successfully. He was now a cardiologist and no longer worked as an intern. Anaya was a happy school teacher and had made quite a few friends in Singapore.

Nishith and Anaya had realized that it would be impossible to live like strangers in the same house, so at least they lived like friends. They still slept in separate bedrooms, but they watched television together, talked about a lot of things and seldom quarrelled. They had learnt to live like friends; the outside world couldn't tell that there was a wall in between. Anaya had accepted the fact that she could never compel Nishith to love her and Nishith had accepted the fact that he had to live with Anaya his entire life despite the fact that he loved Varsha. Nishith still thought he was in love with Varsha and burning away memories of his love from his heart and mind was way too difficult for him. Nishith also understood that torturing Anaya for being the reason of his grief won't curb his sorrow; it only enhanced it further.

Anaya was happy that Nishith had accepted her as a friend, if not a wife. She loved Nishith and her love was stronger that the need for Nishith to love her back. Days passed on with the same flavour until some news from India disturbed the tranquillity.

Anaya was talking to her mother-in-law over webcam one night.

"Hi Mom, when will you come here? We both miss you a lot," Anaya said cupping her face.

"Very soon dear. How are you? How is my son? Hope he doesn't quarrel with you a lot; he is a little short-tempered," Mrs. Chatterjee said as she sipped her tea.

"We are fine, Mom. I can manage his temper now; I am used to it," Anaya said with a smile.

"Oh yes, it's been over four years you both are married. I shouldn't be telling you all this anymore," Mrs. Chatterjee replied with a smile.

"How is Dad?"

"Good. He misses you both a lot. He wants to come there once he gets some good news," Mrs. Chatterjee said with a twinkle in her eyes, which made Anaya feel awkward and uncomfortable.

"Don't feel uneasy, Anu. I know everything, but winds of change will come to your home soon. God bless you," Mrs. Chatterjee said with a feminine care as she saw her daughter-in-law bothered.

"It's because of your wishes that I have settled down well here and Nishith's hatred has grown into friendship," Anaya said recovering quickly from her apprehension.

"Oh yes. He will treat you as his wife very soon and will fall in love with you too. By the way, I had some news to give you. It's about Varsha," Mrs. Chatterjee said seriously.

"Please tell me, Mom. How is Varshu? Is she fine?" Anaya asked.

"Varsha's marriage is fixed to a businessman of Pune. His name is Siddhant Agnihotri. They are getting married day after tomorrow. Varsha's mother called me and invited me to her marriage. So I will be leaving for Bombay tomorrow itself," Mrs. Chatterjee said.

"That's great news, Mom. Varshu is getting married. I wish I could attend her marriage," Anaya said with sheer excitement when suddenly she heard the main door of their house banging shut. She rushed to find Nishith driving away swiftly. Did Nishith hear that Varsha is getting married? Is that why he left the house? Anaya ran to the desktop to tell her mother-in-law what had just happened.

"Oh god! Nishith should not have known this," Mrs. Chatterjee said with knotted eyebrows.

"It's 11 p.m. here, Mom. I am tensed where he could have gone at this hour of the night. What should I do?" Anaya said with consternation.

"Wait for him, Anu. He will be back soon. And drop a message to me as soon as he reaches home," Mrs. Chatterjee pacified Anaya who switched off the computer shortly thereafter. Anaya kept calling Nishith but found his cellphone switched off. It was past midnight but there was no trace of Nishith anywhere. Anaya thought of calling Doctor Uncle for help, and her next door neighbours, but the second thought of clarifying to them the reason for Nishith's reckless behaviour changed her mind. She decided to wait for Nishith quietly as she kept trying his number at frequent intervals. Just when the clock was about to strike two, the doorbell rang. Anaya jumped up, knowing it would be Nishith. She opened the door to find Nishith in a terrible condition. He was badly drunk, his eyes were swollen and red due to profuse crying and he was not even in a condition to stand straight. Anaya got scared to see Nishith in such a state and kept Nishith's hand on her shoulders to help him maintain balance.

"Leave me, Anaya. I can walk myself to my room," Nishith said as his words twisted over his tongue.

"You can hardly maintain your balance, Nishith. How did you even drive back? Let me accompany you to your room, and then I will leave you to yourself," Anaya said and held Nishith.

Anaya removed his shoes and socks as he lay down on the bed in a miserable drunken state. Nishith's shirt was totally wet with alcohol and sweat, so Anaya opened his cupboard and gave him a white kurta to change into.

"Nishith, open this shirt, else you will catch cold," Anaya said sitting beside Nishith whose eyes were still moist.

"Why do you love me so much?" Nishith asked Anaya as she sat beside him.

"You won't listen to me, right? Your shirt is totally dipped in alcohol," Anaya said ignoring Nishith's question as she unbuttoned his shirt.

"You know I can never love you, still just look at you. Why can't you leave me alone?" Nishith said after scanning the way Anaya opened his shirt and wiped his body with her stole.

"Why can't I forget her, Anu? I still love her so much," Nishith got up slowly and held Anaya's shoulders. When she didn't look up at him, he took her into his arms. Anaya felt heavenly as Nishith hugged her for the first time after their marriage. His touch on her body filled her up with ecstasy. She embraced Nishith and could feel his tears falling on her shoulders. Anaya's eyes too welled up as she embraced her husband.

"You go to sleep, Nish. A good sleep will make you feel better. It's already very late," Anaya said breaking the embrace and wiping the tears off Nishith's face.

"Don't go away, please," Nishith said holding her hand as Anaya was about to leave the room.

"But...?" Anaya was about to speak when Nishith removed the strand of hair falling on her face and kissed her lips. The sensation of Nishith's lips on Anaya's felt so entrancing to Anaya that despite her knowledge that Nishith was not in his senses due to over consumption of alcohol, she did not stop him. Anaya gave in to the kiss and kissed Nishith with all her love and passion which had been suppressed in her for the past four years. Both Nishith and Anaya wanted this; they were starving of love. Although alcohol had curbed Nishith's judgment of whether he wanted this, Anaya could not stop herself from surrendering to Nishith with all her mind, soul and body. A woman hungry for her man's love can never stop her man from loving her, touching her and feeling her. Anaya switched off the bedside-lamp and smothered Nishith's body with kisses all over. Nishith fondled, caressed and kissed her back. There was no thread of cloth left on their bodies as their love grew more intense with every passing second and their touches and kisses grew wilder. Both of them touched each other in the darkness of the room, making each other moan with inevitable, undeniable pleasures. They climaxed together, marking each other with their love. They hugged each other like there was no tomorrow and dozed off to sleep.

The rays of sun fell on Anaya's face, breaking her slumber. She found herself locked in Nishith's arms and remembered every detail of the last night. She smiled and kissed Nishith's forehead and got up from the bed. She got herself dressed and loved the smell of Nishith's body on hers. She made two cups of tea and thought of waking Nishith up. As she entered Nishith's room, she saw Nishith had already got ready for the hospital.

"Good Morning," Anaya said as she gave him his cup of tea. Nishith did not reply and ignored her beaming smile. She had not expected this and asked him the reason behind his ignorance. Nishith got agitated.

"I was not in my senses last night, but you were, Anaya. Why did you let that happen between us last night?" Nishith shouted.

"Because I love you. It may be an aberration for you, but it was my love for you which made me make love to you last night." Anaya shouted back as Nishith gave her a deaf ear and walked out of the house towards the hospital.

WINDS OF CHANGE

Anaya sat on the couch surfing through channels mindlessly. She could not put her concentration anywhere and kept looking at her wrist watch every five minutes. Nishith had been aloof for a few weeks after that night, but he had softened towards her thereafter. She dialled Nishith's number quite a few times but was not audacious enough to give him the news she was holding to herself at that time. As time passed, Anaya grew more restless. She thought about that night, Nishith's anger in the morning and her love for him. It was not too cold in Singapore; yet she felt shivers down her spine. She wrapped a shawl over her tee, made a cup of coffee for herself and took long breaths to divert herself. After a while, she heard the horn of Nishith's car and the palpitation of her heart doubled. She opened the door and gave him a silly smile.

"Hey! How was your day?" Nishith asked his wife as he entered the house.

"Very good. Yours?" Anaya said carrying that silly smile.

"As usual. Not as good as yours, I guess," Nishith said as he sat on the couch after removing his blazer.

"Shall I make you a cup of coffee? Or tea? What do you want? Is it too cold today or is it only me who is feeling exceptionally cold?" Anaya blabbered out so many things at once.

"Anaya…are you alright?" Nishith said holding Anaya's hand.

"Yes, I am fine. Why?"

"You seem so lost. You are behaving strangely. What happened? Tell me," Nishith sounded concerned.

"Actually..." Anaya said after a sigh.

"I am getting worried Anu, what is it?"

"I don't know how to tell you, or what to say. I don't know anything," Anaya said rubbing her hands.

"Did they fire you from your job?" Nishith said with a smile.

"What?"

"Well...I am just trying to make you comfortable. So tell me."

"Why will I get fired from my job? I am too good with kids," Anaya said as a smile lit up her face.

"I know that. I was just playing around. So did some handsome foreigner propose to you?" Nishith asked with a twinkle in his eyes, still holding Anaya's hand.

"What rubbish! I am your wife Nishith," Anaya said furrowing her eyebrows.

"Your awkward behaviour made me think so. You don't know what to tell me, how to tell me. So I made a wild guess. And moreover, you are quite pretty to make anyone fall in love with you," Nishith said.

"Is it? It took you a few years," Anaya joked, but Nishith's face turned serious immediately. So she held his hand tighter and said, "It's not that simple, and you stop joking for my sake," Anaya said biting her lower lip.

"Okay, okay! You sit here, on the couch. Stop getting so restless. Take a long breath and tell me." Nishith pulled Anaya by her hand and made her sit on the couch in front of him.

"Nishith…do you like kids?" Anaya asked.

"Of course. I am most attached to my child patients," Nishith said with a smile.

"If a kid starts living in this house, will you be happy?" Anaya asked. "Are you planning to adopt some of your students?"

Anaya shook her head.

"Will you be specific, Anaya? I am bad at solving riddles."

"I went to the hospital today for a check-up," Anaya said slowly.

"Are you sick? You did not even tell me that you will be going to the hospital today," Nishith got hysterical.

"Nishith, listen! And please don't shout else I can't tell you what I want to."

"What happened to you?" Nishith asked putting his hand on Anaya's forehead to check her body temperature.

"Nothing. I don't have fever. I am pregnant," Anaya said removing Nishith's hand.

"What? You are pregnant!" Nishith said, not knowing how to react.

"Yes. I am three-months pregnant," Anaya said with pulsating heartbeat, not looking up at Nishith, scared about his reaction.

"Congratulations!" Nishith said with a smile after thinking for a moment.

"Are you really congratulating me? I thought you would not accept this child," Anaya said with wonder.

"What is this child's mistake that I won't accept him/her? I am happy."

"Are you seriously happy, because you are going to be a father soon?"

"Yes Anaya. I am serious."

"Then congratulations to you too," she finally beamed.

He hugged her lightly and knelt down in front of her, "Thank you so much, Anu. Did you inform Mom and Dad about this news?" Nishith asked.

"I thought to share it with your first. I will inform them now. They will be over whelmed with happiness," Anaya said with sheer joy on her face. In his bedroom, Nishith thought that even though he did not love Anaya, this baby in Anaya's womb was his own blood, his own flesh. No matter how it had happened between them, the fact was that they had made love on that particular night and this baby was a consequence of that night. No one could alter this truth. Moreover, he did not want to be a ruthless human by showing Anaya a deaf ear when she told him that she was carrying his child. Nishith thought of Varsha, and that she was already married. Nishith knew Varsha did not love him ever and Varsha must be very happy in her own life with her husband. Nishith thought of Anaya who had made every possible effort to win his heart in the past four-and-a-half years. Nishith thought of his rudeness and Anaya's generosity and love for him. Anaya did not ever complain against his attitude towards her. She woke up in the dead of the night when Nishith was unwell, she made Nishith's favourite dishes, waited for

Nishith's love all these years and Nishith always abandoned her.

Nishith felt guilty as he thought about his behaviour towards Anaya for all the past years. He went into Anaya's bedroom and saw her sleeping peacefully. Her nose was shining in the dark and she looked cute. Nishith gazed at her face and caressed her cheek gently. Anaya was startled.

"What happened, Nishith? Are you alright? Do you need something?" Anaya asked, springing from her bed.

"Nothing happened. I just can't sleep alone anymore, while my wife sleeps here," Nishith said holding her hands.

"What?"

"I want to take care of my baby and my baby's mother and if we sleep in separate rooms, I won't be able to take good care, you see," Nishith said.

Anaya's eyes welled up as Nishith's words touched the innermost chord of her heart. Nishith lifted her in his arms and carried her to his room their room. As he laid her on the bed, he patted her shoulders and made her sleep.

Nishith felt an unknown peace surrounding him as he started caring for Anaya. He felt happy with the winds of change that greeted him.

AN OBJECT OF SHOCK

Anaya was in her twenty-fifth week of pregnancy; there was roughly two months and a few days left for her delivery. With Nishith's increasing care for her and their baby, Anaya started enjoying this would-be-mummy feeling. She left her job since Nishith had advised her complete home rest. She was in her sixth month and Nishith had asked the library-man to deliver and collect books on a weekly-basis from their house so that Anaya does not need to go to the library all by herself. As the pregnancy advanced, Anaya suffered from heaviness of legs which caused difficulty in sleeping for her. There was also a little swelling in her legs due to worsening of varicose veins.

"It's paining a lot. I can't sleep," Anaya said as Nishith patted her shoulders to make her fall asleep.

"Anaya…do you know our baby is growing in your womb? Her digestive system, cardiovascular system and endocrine glands have become more autonomous," Nishith said as he massaged Anaya's legs which were in pain.

"Really?" Anaya said putting her hands on her womb with amazement.

"Your reports say so. Due to a little problem in circulation, such minor things happen. You don't worry at all," Nishith said with a smile.

"By the way, how do you know the baby is she?" Anaya asked. "I feel so, and moreover, I would love to have a daughter," Nishith said applying some ointment on Anaya's legs.

"I want to see your childhood. So I prefer a son," Anaya said and winked.

Nishith smiled, "Now try to sleep Anaya. Sleeping is very important for an expecting mother; else all sort of negative thoughts will bother you. Do you know what?" Nishith said pulling the blanket up till Anaya's shoulders.

"What?"

"From the next week or the week after, you will be able to feel the slight movements of our baby in your womb. Do tell me whenever she kicks you for the first time," Nishith said excitedly and laughed.

"It will be such a moment of delight when my baby will communicate with me for the first time," Anaya said with a peaceful smile.

"Our baby."

"Of course, our baby," Anaya said with a smile and fell asleep soon.

The next morning, Anaya woke up to her favourite music being played on the music player and a cup of tea which Nishith had made for her. It had become a regular custom for Nishith to wake her up and make tea for Anaya before leaving for the hospital so that she could wake up with a lovely feeling and a smile. Nishith had really become a doting husband ever since he got the news of Anaya's pregnancy. He had also appointed a cook as he strictly forbade Anaya to go in front of fire. On some days, Nishith would also prepare a light breakfast for Anaya, especially the dishes she craved to eat such as Italian pasta, Baked stuffed potato skins, Macaroni and cheese, etc. Nishith had a fascination with Italian and Mexican food and even learned a few recipes Anaya loved.Anaya was living the best years of her life.

After Nishith left for the hospital, Anaya spent her time watching movies or reading some books or writing some articles on an online forum. She has lately got this habit of writing articles on her personal life and personal experiences on an online site. It was known as blogging in contemporary Indian language and through her blogs, she had acquired many readers and followers.

One day, as Anaya was watching one of her favourite movies in the morning, the doorbell rang. The cook summoned her as she opened the door since it was a postman carrying a letter for Nishith from India. Anaya was startled to read the name of the sender written on the envelope. It read Mrs. Varsha Agnihotri. Anaya signed and received the letter on Nishith's behalf and kept looking at the envelope without knowing whether she should read the letter or just keep it on Nishith's table so that he can read it when he returns home. Anaya couldn't fathom why Varsha had decided to write to Nishith after five years of his marriage. For the last five years, Nishith and Varsha had not kept any contact with each other and suddenly this letter was a bolt from the blue.

Varsha's address and contact number were also written on the envelope just below her name. Does that mean Varsha wants Nishith to keep contact with her again, after all these years? Anaya kept thinking about the several causes and consequences of Varsha's letter and after thinking for more than two hours, she made up her mind to read the letter. She knew it was a shameful act to read someone's personal letter, but her own insecurity and gut feeling did not let her breath in peace. Without wasting a single moment, she tore the brown envelope open and pulled out the letter. Her heart beat rose as she started reading the contents of the letter written in red ink.

Dearest Nishith,

I can't believe I am writing to you today. It's been five years that we talked to each other, saw each other's face or even tried to know about each other. There was a time when my day started with you and ended with you, and this is the time when you are not there to hold my hand. Only your memories support me. I am married now. I took your address from Sumona aunty's purse when she came for my wedding. You know Nishith, sometimes we realize things too late and when we do realize, our life becomes an atrocious torture.

When my marriage was fixed and I started my courtship with Siddhant, I started realizing that there was no spark between me and Siddhant. Siddhant is a presentable man, enormously rich and well-behaved. There is hardly any flaw in him, but every time I looked at him, my eyes searched you in him. I thought this was my misinterpretation initially, but even after marriage, I could not forget you. I kept searching you in Siddhant, may be I am still searching you in him.

Am I not a fool, Nish? How can I find you in anyone else? Was I not a fool, Nish? How could I not realize earlier that I loved you? I am in love with you Nishith, always was. I just I realized it too late. You know your Varshu was a tom boy, hated romantic stuff, so how could such a happy-go-lucky-girl possibly believe that she was in love with her best friend? She thought it was friendship and nothing else. With the passage of time, your tom-boy Varshu has ripened to a woman and has realized her love for you from her womanly heart. I know you love me and I can still feel your love for me Nishith. I know you love me and it won't be easy for you to love Anu. I don't want you to opt for a divorce after reading the letter; nor can I leave Siddhant after realizing my feelings for you. I just wanted you to know that the person you were in love with also feels the same and will continue to love you. May be we are not destined to be together; maybe our love story is an unfinished and unaccomplished one. I would be more than glad to hear from you.

Heart-filled love,

Yours Varsha.

Anaya's eyes welled up as she read the letter, not only due to grief but also due to anger and jealousy. *How does it feel for a wife to know that the woman her husband loved suddenly realized that she has the same feelings for him after five years?* Is this not an ugly joke?

Anaya went inside her bedroom and sobbed uncontrollably as she thought of the letter. She was sure that if Nishith read the letter, he will leave Anaya and run to Varsha. Anaya caressed her bulging stomach and thought about her baby who had not even opened its eyes yet. *What would Anaya say to her child about her father? How could she say that her father ran to his childhood sweetheart abandoning both of them?*

The mother in Anaya made her selfish. In a trance, Anaya kept the letter in the locker of her cupboard along with her jewellery. Anaya made up her mind to never say a word to Nishith about this particular letter. More than keeping Nishith to herself, she wanted Nishith for the sake of her baby. *Their baby.* If Anaya would not have been with a child, she would have let Nishith go to his love. The wife in Anaya could have accepted defeat in the face of another woman; but the mother could not.

THE STRONGEST THREAD

When Nishith gave Anaya her regular medicines after dinner, Anaya kept looking at Nishith. Her mind was still on the letter from Varsha she received some ten hours back. A lump started forming in her throat due to the jealousy, unsaid anguish and unexpressed despondency.

"Are you alright?" Nishith asked as he caught Anaya gazing at him without battering an eyelid.

"Do you still love Varsha?" Anaya asked holding back her tears.

Nishith's expression changed and he held Anaya from her shoulders, "Listen to me carefully, Anaya." Anaya bent her face as a teardrop escaped from the corner of her eyes despite her efforts to hide it.

"I admit I had always loved Varsha, but I will be inhuman if I am incapable of loving three people in my life. One, my mom; second, my baby; and third, the woman who bears my child. I have accepted that Varsha is my past; you and our baby are my present and future. So only you and our baby have all the right on my love. Plus, Varsha is married and well-settled in her life. She is my past and will always stay in a small corner of my heart as my first love. Nothing more than that! It is you and our baby whom I love and want to love more and more with each passing day. You get it?" Nishith said holding up Anaya's chin after explaining his feelings gently.

"I love you, Nishith." Anaya said and embraced Nishith. He held her in his arms, assuring her to never worry about such things and that he would always be with her in every condition. Anaya prayed forgiveness from God for hiding the letter from Nishith as she rested her head on Nishith's shoulders.

The next two months flew rapidly with Nishith's parents and Nishith caring for Anaya and the day of delivery knocked finally. Anaya was admitted in the Mount Elizabeth Hospital under Doctor R. Sabharwal who was a friend of Doctor Uncle. The doctor had clarified that Anaya would have to undergo a caesarean since the baby was not lying head down, such as it is in a breech position. Anaya was very nervous when she was finally taken to the operation theatre. She held Nishith's hand and her mother-in-law's hand out of jitteriness.

"Don't be nervous, Anu. You will be given anaesthesia and after that when you will open your eyes, you will see our baby smiling at us," Nishith said, sitting on his knees beside her bed and Nishith's mother caressed Anaya's head.

"I am scared of operations, Nish. You come inside the OT with me. I don't want to be all alone," Anaya started panting.

"Everyone will take care of you, and I am just outside the OT. Be strong dear, for our baby, for our angel," Nishith said brushing his lips softly on Anaya's forehead which made Anaya feel better. She nodded her head and was taken to the OT by the nurses. After one hour, Doctor Sabharwal came out of the OT congratulating the Chatterjee family for their new member, a girl child. He informed that Anaya was unconscious due to the effect of anaesthesia and that they could meet her in a couple of hours.

Nishith was elated and jubilant as he held his daughter in his hands. Nishith kept watching with wonder the tiny fingers, those tiny legs and the small pretty face cringing her nose and closing her eyes every now and then due to the excessive light of the hospital. The baby started crying and Nishith kissed her lovingly with fatherly adoration. Nishith did not miss a single movement of his daughter.

"Nishith, she has lips and nose completely like you," Nishith's mother remarked as she caressed her granddaughter's head.

"But she has got such beautiful lovable eyes from my Anu," Mrs. Chatterjee continued with her remarks.

"Come on, Sumona! She has just stepped into this world and you have started comparing her eyes and lips to our kids. You women are too much," Nishith's father laughed at his wife's remarks.

"Whoever she may look like, Mom, my daughter is so beautiful." Nishith said in awe.

"That is because my son and my daughter-in-law are so beautiful. How can my grand-daughter not be pretty?" Mrs. Chatterjee again continued her remarks.

"Nishith, the baby needs to be kept in the nursery for a few hours. After Anaya come to senses, you take her to Anaya. Till then, there is a list of things which your baby needs. Please get them soon," Dr. Sabharwal ordered and Nishith left with the list.

Anaya woke up a couple of hours later to a faint pain in her lower stomach where the incision has been done. Mrs. Chatterjee caressed Anaya's head and Anaya started asking her about the baby.

"Nishith will be here any moment with your daughter. Thank you, my love," Mrs. Chatterjee kissed Anaya on her forehead and

Nishith entered her cabin with their baby in his hand.

"Oh!" Anaya started smiling with tears of joy as she held her baby in her hands. The baby she carried for nine months, the baby she waited for so long, the baby she had fallen in love with ever since she knew the baby was a part of her.

"Isn't she so cute? My angel," Anaya said looking at Nishith and kissing her daughter lovingly on her cheeks. The baby pouted her lips and smiled as she saw her mother fondling her.

"She is smiling as you kissed her, Anu," Nishith said kissing her daughter and the baby again pouted her lips and broke into a smile. All of them laughed at this cute gesture of their new member.

"Have you thought of any name, Anu?" Mrs. Chatterjee asked as Anaya adored her baby.

"Yes Mom. I have. I want to name her Olivia," Anaya's words startled Nishith and Nishith's parents. They gave a blissful smile as Mrs. Chatterjee had named her daughter Olivia, who had turned out to be a still born child. She had told this story to Anaya years back and Anaya had remembered.

"Thank you for giving me the most beautiful gift of this whole universe," Nishith said embracing Anaya.

"Thanks to you too. I wouldn't have had her alone, you know," Anaya blushed.

"Our baby has got all the beauty from you," Nishith said caressing Olivia who seemed to fall asleep in her mother's arms.

"Oli has fallen asleep," Anaya said with a smile.

"Oli...such a cute nickname! Our Olivia. Miss Olivia

Chatterjee," Nishith pronounced his daughter's name with love, pride and contentment.

"Nishith and Anaya's Olivia," Anaya said looking at Nishith.

"I want to say something, Anu," Nishith said.

Anaya just raised her eyebrows, curious to know what he could have had in mind at this moment.

"I love you, Anu." Nishith finally said those three magical words to Anaya on the day of their daughter's birth. Their daughter truly became the strongest thread of their relation.

"I love you more," Anaya smiled and looked at her daughter who was smiling in her sleep oblivious to the fact that her father had just told her mother the best thing in the world.

TO COVER ONE LIE

Anaya was discharged from the hospital after five days of her delivery and she was taken complete care of by her in-laws and Nishith.

"It's so good to be home," Anaya said to Nishith after putting baby Olivia to sleep.

"Yes it is," Nishith said kissing Anaya on her forehead.

"You seem to be a super happy father. I have never seen you so happy in years," Anaya said to Nishith with a light grin.

"It's because I fell in love with two girls at the same time…my daughter and my wife," Nishith said running his fingers through Anaya's long hair.

"So is this making you such a happy man?" Anaya said playfully.

Nishith pulled Anaya closer to him and showered tender kisses on her lips.

"It is the first time we are kissing in full sense," Anaya said with a laugh.

"Let's make it a second and third and fourth and fifth and uncountable this night," Nishith put his lips on Anaya's lips as he completed saying those words and kissed her again, this time with fervent passion accompanied with dollops of longing. Though Anaya was not supposed to move, thanks to the stitches on the lower stomach, but she responded with ecstasy. It was passionate, unending kissing to make each other feel loved and to love each other madly. As they were lost in kissing each other in the divine moment of desire, Anaya opened her eyes for a second and saw baby Olivia looking at her parents with round eyes. Anaya started laughing at the sight.

"Our daughter has caught us kissing, Nish," Anaya said as Nishith looked at her with a question on his face. Nishith too broke into laughter as he saw baby Olivia looking towards them with big, round, twinkling eyes.

"Oops, mummy and daddy made a boo-boo," Anaya said taking her baby in her lap and the baby started laughing as if she understood every word Anaya had said.

"Our daughter is too smart Anu," Nishith said laughing.

Six months had passed after Olivia's birth and Nishith's parents had left for India. Anaya did not join her job as the articles she had written online had earned her lots of readers, including a few editors and publishers from India who had been asking her to try her hands at writing. Since Anaya has contributed all her time to look after Olivia, she thought this was the best time when she could write a book – sitting at home and taking care of her six-month old at the same time. Nishith encouraged Anaya to chase her dream of becoming a writer too.

Life was blissful till another letter from India disturbed the peaceful ambience around Anaya. Yes, it was another letter from Varsha, sent from the same address. Anaya tore the envelope without hesitation and started reading it with the same rage.

To the only reason why I smile,

I never imagined that you won't reply to my letter. I waited eight months for your reply. Each day of those eight months, I have waited with the hope that you will respond. Why did you not reply, Nish?

You must be very happy with Anu; you may have fallen in her love too. That is great news. I am happy for you if that is the case. You could have written this in the letter. I did not tell you to come to me. I just wanted to hear from you. I miss you. You have moved on in life, but I could not. I am trying to control my tears to fall on this piece of paper as I want to share something with you.

Siddhant is not the guy for me. I discovered two months ago that he is having an affair with a model who works with his agency. When I confronted him, he verbally abused me and slapped me too. I want to run away from his house but I don't want my parents to suffer. Siddhant is an extremely powerful man and he has warned me to not tell the world anything against him.

My life has become a burning torture, Nish. Do you know what makes me smile even today? The memories spent with you since our childhood. Whatever my life is, I want you to be happy always. Be happy with Anu, because she loves you a lot. I am sure you have forgotten me completely and have fallen in love with her. She is so lovable. Perhaps you won't reply to this letter too, but I got a little tranquillity writing to you about my life. You mean so much to me. Your memories have kept me alive even today.

Varshu

The rage Anaya had felt while tearing the letter open turned into pity and sympathy for Varsha by the time she finished reading. Anaya felt pathetic as she read how Varsha's life had turned out. She was stuck in the middle of a loveless marriage where her husband tortured her. Plus, she had discovered her love for Nishith, and though she couldn't do anything else about it, was still waiting for just one letter from him. Anaya made up her mind to give Varsha's letter to Nishith as she wanted her cousin to find some peace. She did not want to snatch the little peace and happiness from Varsha because of her insecurities and selfishness. Anaya remembered Varsha's smile, her liveliness and felt like calling Varsha on the number written on the envelope. With a confused mind, Anaya dialled Varsha's number. After three rings, she could hear Varsha's voice uttering a soft hello. Anaya wanted to speak to her but suddenly, as she looked at baby Olivia crawling on the bed, she realized that she was going to dig her own grave.

She disconnected the phone instantly and ran to baby Olivia and took her in her arms. Anaya hugged the baby and started crying as she thought of Varsha. *I am sorry Varshu. I am so sorry. I can't do this to my baby.* Anaya mumbled these words as she hugged baby Olivia in her arms. Burying this secret deeper into her heart, Anaya kept the second letter inside the locker, with the first one. She could not give the letter to Nishith; the mother in her made her weak once again.

The sea of secrets hidden inside the mantle of Anaya's heart made her become a successful writer. The pain and the secret delving in her heart made her write really well and within two years, Anaya became the author of a published fiction book named *"Understanding a Woman"*.

The book became quite successful in India and her in-laws and Nishith were very proud of her.

***

Since there were no other letters, life was on track. It had been three years and Olivia had started going to school. Anaya had decided to make a career on writing by quitting her job as a school teacher. One day yet again, another letter of Varsha came knocking in Nishith's absence. The letter made Anaya realize that she had to commit a sin once again. That's the truth of life: to cover one lie, you have to say a hundred lies.

Dearest Nishith,

Congratulations! I heard you are a father now. Oh my God... my Nishith has become a dad! I am so glad for you. I have read Anaya's book too. I knew she had this potential of being a writer in her. Remember her diary? Your wife is really talented. And once again, you did not reply to my letter. You must be busy with your daughter and wife. So no complaints with you.

I am writing again after three years to satisfy my soul, without expecting any sort of reply. In true love, there should be no expectation and condition, and you are my one true love. I am in a horrible state Nishith. Day by day, Siddhant's violence towards me has been increasing. He won't give me a divorce; nor will he stop with his affairs. I wish I could be a mother like Anaya but Siddhant has some medical problem, so I am denied that blessing too. I want to adopt a child, but Siddhant's family won't allow me to do that. Worse than that, my in-laws have spread it around the world that I am incapable of giving birth to a child in order to hide their son's incapacity. People look at me with sympathy; middle-aged ladies call me "untouchable" when I go to any ominous ceremony around here.

Life is so unfair to me, Nish. I wish I could just hug you for once and forget all the miseries of my life. Please don't forget me, Nishith. Keep me somewhere in the corner of your heart and in the petals of your memories. I really want to reside there. I love you from every corner of my aching, tattered heart.

Varshu

Once again, Anaya felt suffocated as she read the miseries of her cousin and wished if, only if she could hand over all the letters to Nishith. Anaya cried for the burden of sins she was inflicting herself with, and also for Varsha's sorrows. Anaya felt helpless as she could not do anything for Varsha, despite knowing that only she has the capacity to free Varsha from the grievances of her life.

Nishith made love to her that night, but Anaya embraced Nishith tighter at the fear of losing him.

"Can I ask you something?" Anaya said.

"You don't have to seek my permission," Nishith said pulling Anaya close to him.

"Don't you remember Varsha? Don't you miss her?"

"Well, I should not miss her Anaya. I should not cling to her memories.

That will be injustice to you and Oli," Nishith said seriously.

"It won't be. I am giving you the permission. Don't forget Varsha ever; keep her in one corner of your heart. I won't mind, seriously," Anaya said softly.

Nishith hugged Anaya as her words touched his heart. Anaya asked the Almighty for forgiveness for hiding Varsha's letters from Nishith as he made love to her.

A HEART FULL OF SECRETS

Anaya got Nishith's love, the thing she desired more than anything else on this planet. She had a lovely daughter who was then in class seven and she had a successful career as a writer. Four of her novels had become international bestsellers and she got fame, love and wealth. Having a lovely family and a successful career was like a dream come true. She had been an orphan and had never imagined her life would take such a turn. But then, whenever she thought of Varsha's condition in India and the letters that she had concealed from Nishith, she felt the earth under her consuming her gradually.

The amount of selfishness she exhibited had no mercy; but God had designed a mother this way. A mother could go to any limits for the happiness of her child. Anaya knew she could live without Nishith, but she could not endure the pain Olivia would have suffered if she had to live without a father. Love made people selfish and a mother's love had no limits. Anaya was trapped in the maze of her thoughts as she read the fourth letter she received after eight long years.

Dear Nishith,

When I did not get any reply of my third letter, I decided not to write to you anymore. I assumed that you have moved on in life and you are not ready to look back anymore.

However, my circumstances have compelled me once more to write to you. I am forgetting things, Nishith. I can't remember recently learned things, I can't keep track of things which I have to do. I can't even keep track of time sometimes. I am writing this letter with extreme difficulty under the guidance of my doctor Ritu Singh. I went to her for check-up a week earlier and she told me that I am diagnosed with early symptoms of dementia. I am having memory loss. I want to meet you Nishith, maybe for the last time...what if we meet a few years later and I can't recognize you at all? My life has been an utter failure. I don't have a career, I don't have a loving husband, I don't have children, and I don't have you, my best friend. The doctor here have told me that I will be fine; but my instinct says otherwise. I want to meet you just once, for a few minutes if not more.

Please come to India and meet me Nishith. It is the last wish of your childhood best friend whom you had once loved so dearly. Please let me meet you once, and then, even if I lose my memory for the rest of my life, I won't regret. I want to meet Anaya and your daughter too. Please come to India once...for me...please.

I can't write any more, I don't know what I had wanted to write. I know you will come to meet me. My Nishith can't be so hostile to a dying woman.

Varsha

Anaya sat covering her face with her hands after she read the letter twice. Just then, Olivia came and hugged her from behind.

"Mom, why are you so stressed? Do you need a back massage?"

"No baby. Mom is fine. How was your day at school?" Anaya said kissing Olivia on her cheeks.

"My day was awesome. You know I met Sana's elder sister while coming back from school. She has read all your books and was pleading with me to bring her home so that she could meet you," Olivia said keeping her bag on the bed.

"So what did you tell her?"

"I told her my mom is very busy. I have to seek her permission. After all, you are a celebrity mom. I can't just bring anyone to you," Olivia said with a proud smile.

"My daughter is too smart," Anaya smiled.

"Daughter of a celebrity writer, after all," Olivia winked.

"Stop winking. Bad manners."

"Oh mom, it is so cool to wink. You too wink like me!" Olivia said winking again and again.

"Stop winking, or else you won't be getting your ice-cream today." Anaya said with stern eyes.

"Fine! Dad will bring some more for me," Olivia made a tongue-out face.

"The amount of emoticons you use while texting your friends is lesser than the amount of expression your face carries," Anaya said pulling her daughter close to her.

"That's why I want to be an actress Mom. After school, I want to do film-studies," Olivia said with twinkling eyes. The two pony tails, small oval shaped face, brown twinkling eyes and strawberry lips with a hint of a dimple on her right cheek made Olivia look like a childhood version of some Disney princess.

"Sure baby. Do whatever your heart desires. Now go, change. I am setting your lunch."

After Olivia left the room, Anaya kept the letter inside the locker. Her heart had become an ocean of secrets. Anaya wondered where this secret of hers would take her one day. She was well aware that no matter how much she tried to hide the truth, it would inevitably surface.

She fought her emotions and gathered courage to give Varsha a call. After ensuring that Olivia was taking her nap, she called on Varsha's number. But she was careful to not call her from the house number; she strolled out to the nearest booth and called her.

"Hello," a faint voice greeted Anaya.

"Am I talking to Varsha?"

"Hmm. Who is it?"

"Anaya."

There was an awkward silence for a few minutes. When Anaya was about to disconnect the call assuming the line has got disconnected, she could hear Varsha speaking.

"Anu, from Singapore?" Varsha asked. It seemed that Varsha had taken long to recollect.

"Yes Varsha. How are you?" Anaya said gently.

"Not good Anu. I am dying, both physically and mentally," Varsha's voice cracked after uttering those few words. She started crying as she recognised her cousin's voice with great difficulty.

"I know Varsha. I am so sorry. Please forgive me for everything. I am your sinner." Anaya said with a lump in her throat as she heard Varsha's tears.

"What do you mean Anu? You are so kind to call me today and you are saying that you are my sinner," Varsha said confused.

"I am sorry Varsha. I could not return Nishith to you. I am sorry. Being a mother, it was not easy for me. I could not let my Oli live a life without a father," Anaya confessed her mistakes in a trance.

"What are you saying, Anaya? I don't want to take Nishith from you; I just want to meet him once, for the last time," Varsha said with difficulty.

"Please forgive me. I have hidden everything related to you from Nishith. He does not know anything about your letters. I have read them all and trust me, I prayed for your well-being every day. But for my Oli's sake, I could not take the risk of losing him." Anaya kept saying.

"What? Nishith...." The call got disconnected suddenly to Anaya's surprise. Anaya's confession kept Varsha speechless and shocked to extremity and after the call got disconnected, Anaya realized what she had done. She had confessed the truth to Varsha as she could no longer hold it to herself. Anaya felt like a betrayer who had betrayed her own cousin sister. She now wanted to run to India and ask for forgiveness from Varsha. However, a second thought of abstracting Nishith from her and Olivia changed her mind. She tried to predict the whole matter as a game of destiny and tried to forget everything related to Varsha. Anaya returned home with a sullen face.

"Hey, what happened to you?" Nishith said with shock as he saw his cheerful wife in a sullen face after he opened the door.

Anaya embraced Nishith and started crying on his shoulders, without uttering a word. Nishith was taken aback to see Anaya in such a miserable state.

"I can't lose you Nishith, even if it costs me my whole life," Anaya said clinging to Nishith.

"Why will you lose me, Anu? I love you. Please calm down," Nishith said patting Anaya's back.

"I am sorry," Anaya said between her feeble tears.

"What is going on, Anu? Why are you being sorry and why on earth are you crying like this? Please tell me what the matter is."

"The matter is I love you the most in the world, Nishith."

Nishith took Anaya in his arms and kissed her forehead as Anaya said those words between her tears.

Anaya had confessed to Varsha her mistake, but she could not have shown Nishith the letters at any cost. After that day, Anaya did not receive any more letters from India and as days went, Anaya overcame this feeling of betraying her cousin to a certain limit. Until that day when she met Varsha in Kolkata. Varsha had become a chronic patient of Alzheimer's disease by then. Anaya had tried to suppress the truth inside her for years, but seeing her cousin suffer from total memory loss and being homeless made the mother and wife in her lose. The woman in her could not see another woman of her age in such a miserable condition. Anaya finally made up her mind to hand over all the hidden letters to Nishith and go to India to take care of her cousin, leaving Olivia and Nishith in Singapore.

Anaya knew that it was a life-changing decision. She also knew that all the love that Nishith had for her could convert to irrevocable hatred once he read the letters and came to know about Varsha. But now, at any cost, she was determined to help Varsha in her worst days. Now when the world knew that Varsha was dead and she has nothing left for her in her life. Anaya was happy that she got Nishith's love in her lifetime, she got the happiness of being a mother, and she got fame and love from unknown people all around the world. Now it was time for Anaya to reveal all the hidden truth to her family and try her level best to recover Varsha from her illness. Anaya knew that she was in search of peace. Irrespective of the fact that she got a lot of happiness in her life, but she was devoid of mental peace from the day she started hiding Varsha's truth from Nishith. Anaya wanted to start a new chapter of her life on the journey to seek mental peace.

***

Anaya took a deep breath as she completed writing all the chapters on the Word document named "THE HIDDEN LETTERS". A tear escaped her eyes and fell on the cup of coffee at the thought of leaving her happiness behind in a few hours.

LEAVING BEHIND

Time can be a person's biggest friend, as also a person's biggest enemy. When time was ripe, Anaya had everything and now when time was against her, she had to give up her happiness. Time could make a person, it could break a person, and most importantly, there was no way to control time. Anaya thought about the bizarre game of time as she stirred sugar in three cups of coffee. She knew this would be the last time she was having morning coffee with her husband and her daughter. Anaya was well aware that Olivia would nag her as she would wake her up early in the morning. However, Anaya went to Olivia's room and pulled the curtains of her room, making the sunrays kiss Olivia in her slumber.

"Mom, let me sleep. I slept at 3 in the morning," Olivia said pulling the blanket over her eyes.

"Oli, get up baby. Your Mom wants to have the morning coffee with you today. Get up darling," Anaya kept Olivia's head on her lap and caressed Olivia's hair.

"Is there some special occasion today, Mom?" Olivia said rubbing her eyes. Olivia's words made Anaya smile sadly. Only Anaya knew the reason why this morning was different.

"You ask too many questions, Oli. It's just that your Mom wants to spend some time with you and your Dad. Got it? Now get up and come to the living room fast. I have to wake up your Dad too," Anaya said kissing Olivia's right cheek. Anaya went to her bedroom and saw Nishith sleeping peacefully. *He did not have any idea how his life would change in a few hours. He did not know that he might be compelled to hate the person he loved the most.* Anaya swallowed the lump in her throat as she gazed at Nishith in sleep.

"Good morning, Nishith," Anaya said caressing his forehead.

"Anu, why did you take the pain of waking me up? You have been writing the entire night. You need sleep," Nishith said as he opened his eyes.

"Quiet," Anaya said putting her finger on Nishith's lips.

"I hate it when you don't sleep properly, Anu," Nishith said getting up from the bed.

"I know Nish, but I really want to have the morning cup of coffee with you and Olivia today. Oli is waiting for us in the living room. Please come fast," Anaya said with a smile on her lips in the effort of hiding all her anguish. Nishith followed her to the living room where they found Olivia sleeping on the couch.

"Oli," Anaya tickled her daughter.

"Mom..."

"You slept again?"

"Sorry Mom. I was waiting for you both. I did not even realise when my eyelashes glued together," Olivia said with an innocent puppy face which made her parents smile.

"Oli, tell your Mom to have a good sleep every day. How many hours do you sleep, Anu?" Nishith asked as he sipped his coffee.

"I agree I sleep less, but please my doctor hubby, you don't have to tell your daughter to advise me," Anaya said with a smile.

"Mom, don't you realize how much Dad loves you. He is always worried about your health. I wish I get a life-partner like my Dad," Olivia said looking proudly at Nishith.

"Stop being such a bold lass, Oli," Anaya said trying to fake some anger.

"Oops! Sorry Mom," Olivia said with a tongue-out face.

"Oli and Nish, can I share a small piece of knowledge with both of you?" Anaya said smiling and both Nishith and Olivia nodded their heads in response.

"Well it goes like this: Suppose you have been given a bunch of keys to unlock a door. When your time is good, the first key you will put your hands on will be the key that can unlock the door. When your time is bad, all the keys you will put your hands on will fail to unlock the door. However, you should not be discouraged. You should keep in mind that when your time is unripe, it will be the last key that can unlock the door. So when your time is not at your best, you be at your best. Never lose hope and faith in the divine." Anaya said in a typical writer's philosophical attitude.

Nishith clapped his hands as Anaya finished her words. Olivia looked at her mom with round eyes trying to understand the depth of those words.

"You are a genius, Anu. All your words inspire me," Nishith said looking at his wife lovingly.

"And your encouragement inspires me to produce such words," Anaya said holding Nishith's hand.

"Did you understand what I said, my sleepy-baby?" Anaya asked Olivia.

"Yes Mom, I did. Dad is right; you are genius. And I am proud of you," Olivia said with shimmering eyes.

"No need to feel proud of me, always remember these words in your life. It will let you face every problem of your life with ease." Anaya said and Olivia hugged Anaya from her side. The morning passed in the blink of Anaya's eyes and both Nishith and Olivia went to hospital and college, respectively. Anaya packed her bags and called up Zeeshan who had booked her flight tickets to India. After knowing that her flight was at 4 p.m., she took out all the letters from the locker and kept the letters along with a small note for Nishith on the bed-side table of their bed-room.

Nish,

I am leaving home. Why I am leaving, you will get to know as you will read these letters which I have kept hidden from you for the last eighteen years. I know my mistake has no mercy, but if you ever want to know the truth behind my mistakes, check your email. I have mailed you a word document named "The Hidden Letters". Take care of yourself and Oli. Call me if you want to know anything about Varsha. I will be with her as soon as I reach India.

Anu.

Anaya had mailed the word document to both Nishith and Olivia. Before leaving the house, Anaya felt like leaving a note for Olivia as well. Olivia would really be perplexed by the sequence of events and after Nishith would read Varsha's letters, Nishith would not be in a perfect state to explain anything to Olivia. Anaya went inside Olivia's room and saw the huge laminated picture kept above Olivia's bed – Nishith and Anaya kissing Olivia's cheeks. Anaya realized that she had to leave her flesh, her Olivia behind too. Anaya wished if she could take Olivia with her, but Anaya did not want to be selfish enough to separate Olivia from her father, her house and her friends. With a heavy heart, Anaya took a paper and pen from Olivia's study-table and wrote a few sentences with tear-laden eyes.

My baby,

Mom is so sorry to leave you here and go to India without telling you. Please don't cry and don't ask Dad why I left home. I have left an e-mail for you, read it if possible. I don't know how much you will be able to comprehend things, but time is hostile to your Mom right now. Pray to God so that time becomes ripe soon for your Mom and Dad. I love you the most in this world.

Take care.Mom.

Anaya wiped her tears as she completed writing the note for Olivia. She took a deep breath, carried her two bags, looked at her house for one last time and walked outside her apartment with a heavy, grief-struck heart. Anaya took a cab and reached the Singapore Airport where Zeeshan was waiting for her with her flight ticket.

"Are you alright?" Zeeshan said with a sympathetic face.

"Never been better," Anaya said with sarcasm.

"Think once again, Anaya. You still have the time to go back to your happiness," Zeeshan said.

"On one side, I have peace. On another, I have happiness.

I have chosen happiness over peace for the last eighteen years. Today, I want to choose peace at the cost of happiness. Don't make me weak, Zee," Anaya said with a struggling smile.

"Call me whenever you need any help. I am always there for you," Zeeshan said holding Anaya's shoulders.

"I know Zee. Take care of my daughter. Try to meet her and explain things which she is unaware of. Please be with my Oli. It's a request. Call me every day and give me updates about Oli. You will do this for me...won't you?" Anaya said worried.

"Anything for you Anaya! You don't worry about Olivia at all. I will take care of her."

"Thanks. Bye!" Anaya said and walked inside the airport leaving behind her soul, her happiness and her life in search of peace. Anaya wanted to help a homeless, memory-less woman of her age, who she had spent half her childhood with, and who has suffered a lot because of Anaya's selfishness and her own malicious fate. Anaya had no control over anyone's fate except the fate of her characters, but she indeed had control over her decisions. She had made a firm decision that she would try her level best to recover Varsha from her illness, at the cost of everything. Anaya took out the family photograph and looked at it with sad, pitiful eyes as the flight took off from Singapore and headed towards India.

A NEW REASON

After landing at the Kolkata Airport, Anaya took a cab straight to the Howrah Mental Asylum. Anaya signed the papers of Varsha's discharge and took Varsha with her to her in-laws' house. Though Varsha was reluctant in the beginning, not recognising Anaya at all, her cajoling and good words helped Varsha regain her composure and accompany her. Anaya's mother-in-law was startled to see Varsha with Anaya, and that too in such a terrible condition.

"Anu, what is going on? How and where did you find Varsha? And how are you here so suddenly?" Mrs. Chatterjee was perplexed to see Anaya shielding Varsha.

"Ma, please give me a few minutes. I will explain everything," Anaya said and took Varsha inside the bedroom. Varsha sat on the bed with sullen eyes, knowing not what to do, how to react and what to say. She kept staring at the wall in front of her. Anaya dug into the refrigerator and used some wheat bread and vegetables to make Varsha a nice sandwich. She wanted to make noodles for her like old times, the times when Varsha was hungry and still too lazy to make some for herself, but looking at her state, she thought Varsha would do better with some healthy food.

"Varshu, open your mouth. See I have a yummy sandwich for you. You have forgotten, but I still remember the time when

I used to make up quick snacks for you in our college days. You were so lazy that you never used to go into the kitchen," Anaya said looking at her cousin who had forgotten every known person of her life. Anaya tried to control her emotions while feeding Varsha and her mother-in-law stood beside Anaya, shocked and petrified with the sequence of events. Mrs. Chatterjee kept talking to Anaya in gestures about Varsha but Anaya ignored her mother-in-law as much as possible. After feeding Varsha, Anaya changed Varsha's dowdy clothes into a tidy suit she dug out of her own suitcase. Though Varsha's thin torso didn't quite fill in to the suit, she was at least dressed in clean clothes now. Anaya prepared the bed for Varsha and tried to make her sleep.

"Go to sleep, Varshu. Don't be scared, your Anu is right here for you. Close your eyes and try to sleep," Anaya told Varsha to lie down and Varsha kept looking at Anaya with pale eyes, without blinking. After a few minutes, Varsha fell asleep. Anaya switched off the lights and went to the living room where both of them were waiting for her.

"Anu, will you tell us now what the matter is? What happened to Varsha? Where did you find her? And how did you come to India so suddenly? Where are Nishith and Oli?" Nishith's mother asked with worried eyes.

"Does Nishith know that you are here Anu?" Nishith's father threw another bullet towards Anaya. He had known her long enough to read her body language.

"Mom, Dad....please relax. Varsha is a chronic patient of Alzheimer's disease and I have brought her to our house from the Howrah Mental Hospital just now. Tomorrow I will take her to the Dignity Dementia Day Care Centre. Then whatever the doctor will tell me to do for her, I will do that. And I have a request...Please don't ask me any more questions. I am sorry I won't be able to answer you. Since I know you treat me like your daughter, I have come here, Dad. I didn't know where to go in such times. Please trust me, and don't ask me why or how I came here," Anaya said folding her hands.

"Anu, this is your house. You can come here whenever you want. You don't have to give us any explanations. I think you should take some rest. It's already midnight," Nishith's father said to Anaya.

"Thanks Dad, thanks for trusting me," Anaya said and walked out towards her room. Anaya stood in the balcony of her room in solitude when her mother-in-law patted her back.

"Mom, please go to sleep. I want to spend some time alone," Anaya said with a choking throat.

"Anu, you are my daughter. I have never treated you as my daughter-in-law. I can see an enormous amount of agony in your eyes; I can hear tears in your voice. I can't be at peace dear. Please tell me what the matter is. Did you leave your house at Singapore? Is everything alright between you and Nishith?" Mrs. Chatterjee asked gently, touching Anaya's cheeks. Though Anaya tried her level best to maintain her strong demeanour, the motherly touch melted her apparent strength. Anaya could no longer resist the tears as she embraced her mother-in-law with her grief-burdened heart. Mrs. Chatterjee held Anaya close to her and caressed gently with motherly tenderness as she could feel her daughter-in-law's emotional trauma.

Anaya wiped her tears and released herself from her mother-in-law's arms after a few painful minutes. Anaya narrated the whole story to her mother-in-law from the day she had met Varsha in Kalighat Temple and her decision of handing Nishith all the letters as she could no longer conceal such a big truth. Mrs. Chatterjee patiently listened to Anaya as she told her that looking after Varsha and helping her recover from her illness was her only aim now.

"You are telling me that you took this decision to get some peace of mind. Tell me one thing Anu, if Nishith hates you after reading those hidden letters, can you survive your entire life with Nishith's hatred for you? What have you not done to gain Nishith's love? And now, when Nishith loves you so much, why did you take such a life-changing decision, my dear?" Mrs. Chatterjee said with worried, moist eyes behind her spectacles.

"I can't let Varsha die, homeless, memory-less, Mom. I have humanity left within me too," Anaya said brushing aside the thought of Nishith's hatred towards her.

"God bless you, Anu. I will pray to God for you." Mrs. Chatterjee kept her hand on Anaya's head and went to her room leaving Anaya in the room with Varsha. Sleep totally eluded Anaya as she kept thinking of Nishith's reaction in Singapore and Olivia's condition on not finding Anaya home. Anaya looked at Varsha and thought about those days when Anaya and Varsha had stayed together in her uncle's house. Varsha used to be such a chirpy effervescent person back then; now she did not recognize anyone, not even herself. All such thoughts somersaulted in Anaya's head in such a brutal way that she barely slept for a couple of hours. It was 4 a.m. when Anaya woke up to a deadly nightmare. After splashing some water on her face, Anaya regained some composure. She went to the balcony where she could see the dark violet sky preparing itself for a brand new day. The freshness of the morning air and the calmness of the dawn made Anaya feel somewhat better. Singapore was ahead of India by one hundred and fifty minutes and Anaya dialled Zeeshan's number after calculating Singapore's time to be somewhat near 7 a.m.

"Hey Anaya! How is everything there?" Zeeshan received the call on the very first ring.

"Were you waiting for my call with your phone in hand? Everything is fine here, Zee," Anaya replied with a sad sigh.

"Yes, Anaya. I could not sleep last night. I was expecting a call from you. Olivia came to my house last night, crying. She told me that Nishith had kept himself locked inside his room. Olivia had pleaded him to open the door, but to no avail. Olivia could not bear her father's indifferent attitude towards her along with her mother's leaving the house all of a sudden. She is only eighteen years old, after all," Zeeshan took a pause.

"What did you tell her? Where is Oli now? Please take care of my daughter, Zee," Anaya said hysterically.

"I told Oli to read your e-mail and I have also assured her that I will take her to you. I dropped Oli at her friend Rishi's house last night. She wanted to spend some time with her best friend. You don't worry, Anaya. I am always there with Oli. I will meet her today and update you," Zeeshan explained.

"Thanks a ton, Zee. And if it's not too much trouble, can you please check on Nishith too," Anaya thought about Olivia as she disconnected the call. How could Nishith have been so indifferent towards their daughter? Maybe Nishith required some time to adapt himself to the long-hidden truth; maybe Nishith had himself got torn after knowing Varsha's current condition. A lot of things came to Anaya's mind, but she collected these jumbled thoughts slowly.

When the sun rose, Anaya helped Varsha bathe, get ready and then took her to the Dementia Day Care Centre. After the doctor had his thorough check-up, he told Anaya to meet him in his personal cabin.

"These patients should not hear anything related to them, so I asked you to meet me here in private. By the way, Mrs. Chatterjee, when was your cousin first diagnosed with Alzheimer's disease?" The doctor asked Anaya.

"Six to seven years back, if I am not wrong," Anaya said calculating the year when she had got Varsha's letter.

The doctor nodded his head in distress and started speaking.

"Alzheimer's disease is a type of progressive deterioration of the structure and function of the brain. It has both a genetic and an environmental component. The genetic component is very strong in the case of your cousin. There are five stages of this disease – prodromal, mild, moderate, moderately severe and severe. Unfortunately, your cousin is currently in the moderately severe state. She has crossed the prodromal, mild and moderate stage over these years without any medication."

"Won't she get recovered from this illness, doctor?" Anaya said clutching her hands.

"In moderately severe stage, there is no such medication, Mrs. Chatterjee," The doctor said regretfully.

"Please doctor, I have come to you with great hope. Please don't disappoint me," Anaya said folding her hands.

"Look, Mrs. Chatterjee, to tell you something in the medical jargon, acetylcholine is one of the several neurotransmitters in the brain. Reduced level of acetylcholine in the brain is believed to be responsible for some symptoms of Alzheimer's disease. So I will prescribe your cousin a few medicines to take care of that, but I can't guarantee her recovery since she is currently in a moderately severe state." The doctor said with gentleness to calm down Anaya.

"Thanks doctor. Is there anything which I can do for her well-being?" Anaya asked.

"Take her to known places, to known people. Talk to her normally, make her talk, play any musical instrument or songs which she liked, make her follow a healthy life-style and shower abundance of love on her. In a known ambience among known people and among warmth and love, she will feel secure and good. The deterioration of her brain structure and function can take a halt. Rest, pray to God for a miracle and give her the medicines I am prescribing now. That's all we can do for her right now," the doctor said, giving Anaya some hope to cling to.

"Thanks a lot!" Anaya said as she took the prescription from the doctor and walked towards the check-up room to take Varsha along with her. Anaya felt horribly guilty as she realized that Varsha is in the second last stage of her disease. Had Anaya taken this decision a few years back, Varsha could probably have recovered from this illness. Tears trickled down Anaya's eyes as she saw Varsha sitting like a corpse on the bench. Anaya hugged Varsha and uttered a feeble sorry through her trembling lips.

MAKING AMENDS

Anaya decided to take Varsha to her parents' house in Mumbai, so that Varsha could get a homely ambience, love and warmth of her own parents. Anaya knew it well that Varsha's parents had accepted that Varsha was no more in this world after she got missing three years back. It would be the best thing Anaya could do for her uncle and aunt as well as for Varsha. Anaya decided to take the first flight to Mumbai after she came back from the dementia clinic with Varsha. Anaya's mother-in-law was not too happy to see Anaya oblivious to her happiness, and making Varsha her top priority, in turn evading her own family.

"Anu, think once again. Varsha's condition won't get any better. Isn't that what the doctor said? What has happened to her is irreversible. Why are you killing your happiness with your own hands?" Nishith's mother said to Anaya as Anaya was about to leave for Mumbai.

"Mom…I know what you are trying to tell me, but I can't leave Varsha alone. She is my responsibility until Nishith comes to India," Anaya explained.

"Oh goodness!" Mrs. Chatterjee said touching her forehead.

"Don't worry too much, Mom. I will be fine. Bless me so that I can fight bravely against every odd," Anaya said touching her mother-in-law's feet. She left for the airport soon after, with

Varsha. The flight took off from Kolkata and Anaya thought of every possible reaction that could come from Varsha's parents on seeing Varsha after so many years. Anaya reached her uncle's house with Varsha, the house which she had last seen years back. The house where Nishith used to live could also be seen from the gate. It brought back an avalanche of old memories. The memories of the first time she had met Nishith came crawling to her eyes. Anaya took a deep nostalgic sigh and looked at Varsha, who was looking at her own house like a stranger. Varsha could not recognize her own house and perhaps she won't be able to recognize her parents too, Anaya thought.

Anaya smiled at Varsha and told her, "Hey Varshu, look where we have come! This is your own house; we are going to meet uncle and aunty soon. Your aayi will be so delighted to see you." Varsha kept looking at Anaya with a confused face, unable to comprehend her words. Anaya held Varsha's hand and rang the doorbell of the house. An old man opened the door. Since Anaya was seeing him after almost twenty-three years, she had a little difficulty recognising him. The old man also had difficulty in identifying Anaya. He would have surely recognised Varsha had she not been hiding behind Anaya.

"Uncle, do you recognise me? I am Anaya," she said with awkwardness, hoping against hope that the old man was indeed her uncle. He had aged tremendously, half with time and more with pain for his daughter.

The old man kept looking at Anaya furrowing his eyebrows, without any words. Within few minutes, an old lady came to the door who greeted Anaya with a smile.

"Anu?"

Anaya nodded her head in response when she understood that the old lady is her aunt.

"Yes chachi. Uncle, it's me, your Anu," Anaya tried to make her uncle realize her identity but the old man quietly went inside the house without a word.

"Please wait, don't go in. I have not come here alone. I have brought the most precious thing of your life to you," saying this, Anaya pulled Varsha from behind, who looked at her mother with perplexed eyes, still clinging to Anaya.

Varsha's mother looked at Varsha with shock written all over her face, unable to believe that her daughter who she had believed dead for so many years was standing alive in front of her eyes. She hugged Varsha with an outburst of emotions. Anaya saw the scenario with sad, pitiful eyes.

"Look, our Varsha is alive," Varsha's mother took Varsha to her father who was equally shocked on seeing her dead daughter alive. Emotions were expressed unrestrained as the old parents met their daughter after three long years.

"Anu, where did you find Varsha? Thank you so much dear for giving us our life." Varsha's mother said to Anaya, holding her hands. Anaya narrated to her uncle and aunt how she found Varsha in the Kalighat temple, as also about the current state of Varsha's disease and what the doctor has advised Anaya to do for Varsha.

"It will be the best for Varsha to stay at her parent's house amidst all the love and warmth. She could start remembering things. She has stayed all these years in an asylum amidst unknown people which has hampered her health. So I thought of giving Varsha the homely ambience; that is why I brought her here to both of you."

"We will do everything possible to bring back her memory, Anu. Thank you so much dear. Varsha's father has stopped talking to people after he came to know about Varsha's missing report." Her aunty pointed at the old man, who was now beaming and looking at Varsha unblinkingly. "You don't know what you have done for us, Anaya. God bless you."

Anaya felt the sword of guilt jabbing her heart as she realized that Varsha's present condition is partly because of her selfishness. Varsha could not recognize her parents properly and started crying as she saw the old lady crying in front of her. Anaya pacified Varsha and after a while, Varsha seemed happy and relaxed in the company of her parents. Varsha did not feel scared in her house and felt peace when her mother hugged her or caressed her. After giving Varsha her medicines for the night, Anaya went to take some rest. She had barely slept for four hours in the last two days. As Anaya closed her eyes, her phone rang. It was Nishith. Anaya held her breath and tried to talk, curbing down the nervousness in her tone.

"Hello Nishith!"

"Where is Varsha?" Nishith asked Anaya bluntly without asking anything about her.

"She is with me in Mumbai at her parents' house. Listen Nishith…" Anaya was about to continue the conversation when Nishith disconnected the call, much to Anaya's disbelief. A detestable, horrible feeling wrapped Anaya as she thought of Nishith. She felt Nishith did not care for her anymore, now that he had the letters. All his love had just died with those letters. Why did people say these words "I love you"? It's too easy to say these few words. But if someone makes some mistakes, these words lose all existence just like that. There is no such love which is unconditional, except the love of parents. All kinds of love come with conditions applied. Anaya kept thinking about the irony of love with a loathsome, abominable heart.

The next morning, as the doorbell rang, Anaya found Nishith standing there, haggard and sleep deprived from his appearance. Nishith looked at Anaya bitterly as he entered the house.

"Where is Varsha? How is she now?" Nishith asked Anaya in a bitter tone.

"She is sleeping. She is not fine; she is in the second last stage of Alzheimer's disease. Doctor has given her some cholinesterase inhibitors and told me to keep her in a homely environment amidst love and warmth," Anaya said looking at the window.

Nishith did not reply and walked inside the room where Varsha was sleeping. Varsha's parents had heard the doorbell and felt awkward seeing Nishith there.

Nishith saw Varsha bundled up on bed, and his heart broke. He caressed Varsha's head and whispered softly in her ears.

"Varshu, look your Einstein is here. Your Nish has come to meet you, Varshu. Don't be such a sleep-bug. Get up, fatty!"

Varsha opened her eyes and got frightened to see Nishith in front of her. She kept looking at Anaya with confused, frightened eyes.

"What are you looking there for? Can't you recognize me, Varshu? It can't be. Stop being such a drama-queen," Nishith kept talking to Varsha with a choked throat as he realized Varsha could not recognize him at all. Nishith looked at Varsha as Varsha went to the corner of the bed, scared of him. His eyes welled up as he saw Varsha in such a terrible condition.

"I met you after more than twenty years Varshu and I never had the slightest idea that when we will meet one day, you will not remember me at all." Nishith walked out of the room.

Anaya was sad to see Nishith and Varsha, who could not recognize her love. Anaya remembered Varsha's letter where she had written to Nishith to meet her once before she loses all her memory. Anaya repented thinking if only she would have given Nishith the letters a few years back. Anaya went to Nishith and touched his shoulder nervously.

"Nishith, please don't break down. Varsha has not been able to recognize her parents also. We will try our level best to bring back her memory. Please be strong."

"Just stay away from me, Anaya. I can't bear to look at you,"

Nishith said without looking at her.

"What? You can't bear to look at me?" Anaya said, hurt by Nishith's venom-stained words.

"No, I can't. You have betrayed me and Varsha like no one ever did. Just stay away from me and, if possible, from Varsha too."

"I did not betray you or Varsha. Didn't you read my e-mail?"

"I did not have any time to waste reading your mail. All my time is for Varsha now. You are only the mother of my daughter and no one else to me," Nishith had no mercy for her.

"Stop being so cruel, Nishith," Anaya pleaded.

"Did you stop with your cruelty when Varsha was pining to meet me just once? You know I did the biggest mistake of my life by marrying you. Just stay away from me now." Nishith left Anaya emotionally paralyzed.

Anaya went inside her room, sad that Nishith had claimed to know her so well, but still had not even tried to know the reason behind Anaya's cruelty. He did not even read her e-mail to know the reason behind hiding those letters from him. Anaya felt a huge hole punctured in the mantle

DISTANCE

Despite staying in the same house, there was an unseen distance between two hearts, that of Anaya and Nishith. They never talked to each other on any subject except that of Varsha. Two months had passed just like that and Varsha's condition had showed no improvement. The good thing was that Varsha did not fear Nishith anymore, as Nishith always spent time with her. It seemed that she felt better in Nishith's company as Nishith showed her their childhood pictures, talked about their childhood memories and tried to make her laugh. Anaya played the piano for her and sang lullabies to her before Varsha's sleeping time. Both Nishith and Anaya made every possible effort to keep Varsha in peace and protection. Yes, they had succeeded to a certain extent too, as Varsha did not fear anyone in her house, she smiled sometimes, though very seldom. But above all else, despite all these efforts, the functioning of her brain had failed to show any improvement.

It was a bright Sunday morning when Nishith was combing and tying Varsha's hair sitting on the terrace. He talked to her about the day when she had danced in her college function on *"Ek do teen"* more than two decades back.

"Do you know Varsha that you were dancing better than Madhuri that day? My young heart was completely falling for you as I saw you dancing with grace and elegance with that lovely pretty dress of yours. I was whistling so badly on that day that everyone thought me to be a local goon instead of a medical student," Nishith showed Varsha pictures of that day.

"See, you are looking so pretty and I am looking so below-average in front of you," Nishith laughed at his words and Varsha kept looking at the photograph thoughtfully and then again looked at Nishith's face with the same thoughtful expression.

"Varshu, what are you thinking, my dear?" Nishith said caressing Varsha's right cheek when suddenly Varsha uttered with trembling lips "Nish..."

"Yes Varshu, try to remember. I am your Nish, your Einstein. Look at me," Nishith felt as if he had won some trophy as he saw Varsha reacting on taking his name. Varsha kept looking at Nishith with tear-laden eyes and embraced Nishith impulsively.

"Can you recognize me, Varshu? Say something more, please," Nishith said taking Varsha in his arms.

"We...are...meeting...after...so...many years. I...missed.... you...Nish," Varsha said these words with a lot of difficulty. Nishith could not believe that he had succeeded in making Varsha recognize him.

"Yes, my Varshu. I missed you too. Please get well soon dear," Nishith said choking on his tears.

Varsha nodded her head with tear-laden eyes and hid herself in Nishith's arms again. Anaya watched the reunion of two old hearts with uneasiness. Anaya was happy with Varsha recognizing Nishith, but the picture of her husband hugging his first love in front of her eyes was like an axe chopping Anaya's heart to a million pieces. Anaya hid herself in the staircase and cried her heart out. Nishith's screams brought her back to reality.

"Varsha! Varsha!! Talk to me..."

Anaya rushed in Nishith's direction to find Varsha lying unconscious in Nishith's arms. "What happened to her? Take her inside the room. I am calling the doctor," Anaya said to Nishith and called up the doctor who was treating Varsha in Mumbai.

The doctor arrived shortly thereafter but Varsha was still unconscious. Nishith was in a state of disarray, though. "Doctor, Varsha recognized me. She spoke some words addressing me. I have not heard her speaking so much since the last two months. But soon after, she fainted in my arms. What's wrong, doctor??" Nishith asked with trepidation.

"Dr. Chatterjee, whenever Alzheimer's patients drift from one stage to the next, they behave in such a manner. Moreover, your continuous efforts must have had an effect on her. She recognized you, but only for few minutes. After she regains her senses, don't even expect her to remember anything that happened in the morning."

"What?"

"I am extremely sorry to say that Varsha's slip in memory only shows her having tripped into the last stage of Alzheimer's. She will slowly lose the ability to walk, sit, or smile. Her brain now appears unable to tell the body what to do. Urinary and faecal incontinence will also occur. She can even forget to swallow her food properly. As the disease will progress, weight loss and bedsores will also be prominent. I suggest you hospitalise her, it will be very difficult for you to do anything for her now," the doctor said regretfully.

"Is there no possible treatment for her now?" Anaya asked as Nishith sat on the chair holding his forehead in grief and shock.

"The only treatment left to apply is the Stem Cell Therapy.

I can't guarantee you the chances of success but stem cell therapy can heal damaged fibers and rejuvenate failing cells during cell division, a process in which they multiply indefinitely. The functioning of her brain cells can heal to a certain extent using the stem cell therapy," the doctor explained.

"Great! I am ready to do anything for Varsha. Where is the best stem cell treatment available in India? I will take her tomorrow itself. I want my Varsha to recover; I can't let her die doctor," Nishith said without hiding his emotions as he looked at Varsha who was still unconscious.

"Well, I would suggest you to take her to the Adiva Stem Cell Centre in New Delhi. They provide you with the best stem cell treatment." The doctor said giving Nishith all the contact details and reference.

The doctor was correct; after Varsha regained her senses, she could no longer recognize Nishith. She was quiet and sullen, more than usual. Nishith made up his mind to take Varsha to New Delhi the very next day so that the stem cell therapy could begin as soon as possible.

"Nishith, I want to talk to you," Anaya said as she saw Nishith packing his clothes and Varsha's medicines and clothes. Nishith did not give her an answer and behaved as if he did not hear anything.

"Stop being so insane. I am your wife, Nishith. We have been married for more than twenty years. We have an eighteen-year old daughter. You can't behave as if I don't exist," Anaya said angrily.

"Yes, I know. You are the mother of my eighteen-year old daughter and that's about it."

"I am your wife too."

"No, you are not."

"Then give me a divorce."

"I will, as soon as Varsha's condition is stable. I can't live with a selfish person like you," Nishith said bluntly.

"For God's sake, stop blaming me, Nishith. You hardly tried to know the reasons why I did what I did. All this poison that you have for me, I did all this for your daughter."

"Oh really? Don't blackmail me taking Oli's name. What you did, no enemy does that. And Varsha is your cousin!"

"Fine! I am the worst person of this planet. I will give you a divorce if that is what you want."

"I only want Varsha to recover and nothing else," Nishith said with an agony in his voice.

"I know. I just wanted to tell you that I will also go to Delhi with you. Varsha needs me; she needs a female companion," Anaya explained.

"We don't need you, Anaya. Varsha is my responsibility; I will take care of her."

"Why are you being so stubborn? Try to understand: Varsha needs me."

"If she needs you, I will call you there. You don't have to go tomorrow. And now, please just leave me alone. I want to take some rest as we have the morning flight," Nishith said and pretended to be asleep as Anaya stood and watched him. Anaya did not want to compel Nishith anymore, to take her along with him. She knew Nishith could be too stubborn at times. Anaya just prayed for Varsha's well-being and Nishith's state of mind as she tried to sleep. She also prayed to God to curb the distance between her and Nishith as she could not bear Nishith's indifference towards her. She missed Oli so much. She had not seen her for two months now. Although she had spoken to her over phone, and knew she was safe with Zeeshan, a bitter taste of distance and separation choked her throat.

SOUL MATE

Two weeks had passed since Nishith took Varsha to New Delhi with him for the stem cell therapy. Nishith did not even call Anaya once to inform her about Varsha's health and condition. He changed his number after he went to Delhi, so Anaya could not contact him by any means. After waiting for a period of two weeks, Anaya felt it was useless for her to wait in Mumbai for Nishith and Varsha. Nishith had made Varsha the only priority of his life and Anaya did not mean anything to him. It was better for Anaya to accept the harsh reality life had kept in front of her, than to wait for Nishith and his forgiveness. When life keeps no other options for us, it's better to move on.

Anaya decided to go back to Singapore to her own house and meet her daughter. She had a career, friends and her daughter there. Though Anaya was doubtful about Olivia's reaction on seeing her, a small part of her heart kept consoling her that Olivia would understand her mother. Anaya was happy that she could at least give Varsha's responsibility to Nishith and Varsha could spend her last days with the person she loved dearly.

Yes, it was bitter to mention the word last for her Varshu, but after researching on the Internet about Alzheimer's disease and talking to several doctors about dementia, Anaya understood that patients could not recover. Of course the disease could be made dormant or inhibited temporarily by the stem cell therapy, but permanent recovery of this illness had not been found in the medical dictionary. Anaya did not want to interfere between Nishith and Varsha; she knew that Varsha was in the safest hands possible. Anaya realized that her role had ended in both Nishith's life and Varsha's. It was time for her to pick up the pieces of her broken, tattered heart and move forward in life. There was no point in regrets or tears over what had happened; the mistakes she did in her life were implacable but she tried her level best to pay for those mistakes. Nothing more was there in her hands; she was human, after all. Anaya met her in-laws before leaving India and told them everything that had happened between Nishith and her in the past few months in Mumbai.

"Our marriage is over, Mom, but my relation with both of you will never end. I will always remain a daughter to both of you and you both will be my parents forever." Anaya said with a pale smile.

"What will happen to Oli? I will talk to Nishith; we will make him understand to not end this marriage," Nishith's Dad said thoughtfully.

"Nothing can be achieved by compulsion, Dad. Varsha is Nishith's first love and watching his first love suffer because of his wife is intolerable to him. It's not his fault, Dad." Anaya explained.

"I wonder how strong your love for Nishith is. Whatever he has done with both you and Oli without understanding you at all, not even making an effort to understand...it is so unacceptable. Varsha is his first love but you are his life-partner, his wife and his true love. No matter how powerful one's first love is, it is nothing compared to the true love, the love which is meant to be. Even after all these, you have no grudges against my son. He is such a fool to leave you, Anaya. And I am very proud of you. I am proud that I loved you like my own daughter ever since I met you," Nishith's mother said looking at Anaya with moist eyes.

"Thanks for your overwhelming support, Mom and Dad. I only know that if our love is meant to be, and if my love for Nishith is true, he will return to me one day. If not, then I will spend the rest of my life with his memories. I am happy that he is the father of my daughter; we have spent more than twenty years as a happy family. All those memories will provide oil to the lamp of my life. You both take care and I love you lot." Anaya said and hugged her mother-in-law before leaving for the airport.

After Anaya landed in Singapore, an avalanche of emotions wrapped her. She had not talked to her daughter for so long; she had only taken updates about Olivia from Zeeshan. She didn't know what Olivia thought about her mother after all that had happened. Did Oli think that her mother was an extremely selfish woman? Did Olivia feel that because of her mother, her father has moved away from her? Did Olivia hate her mother the same way her father had started hating Anaya? All these questions ran in Anaya's head, making her feel sick and terrible. Anaya thought of meeting Zeeshan before going to her house but the constant dizziness she felt made her crave for some rest in her house. Anaya entered the house using the extra key she had with her. There was no one in the house and Anaya went to her bedroom with small steps. She switched on the lights and as she saw her bedroom, a plethora of emotions washed over her. She remembered the countless moments that Nishith and she has spent in the room followed by the harsh realization that their marriage was over. Nishith would never come back to this house and they would never stay under the same roof again. Anaya switched off the lights and sat on the bed covering her mouth; soft cries of her wounded heart filled the room. After a short while, Anaya heard footsteps. They were approaching her. Just then, someone switched the lights on.

"Mom..." Olivia uttered as she saw her mother crying to herself, sitting on the bed.

"Oli...my baby...How are you dear? Your Mom is very sorry, baby," Anaya said between her tears, which became heavier as she had seen her daughter after so many days.

Olivia came running to Anaya and embraced her mother with as much vigour as her slim body could produce. Olivia started crying too as she felt her mother's pain in her heart.

"Please don't cry, Mom. I am with you, always with you," Olivia said these words gently as she hugged her mother. These few words seemed to breathe in a new life within Anaya. Anaya feared that her daughter would reject her too, but hearing her daughter say that no matter what, her daughter is on her side always, filled Anaya with a ray of hope.

"Really?" Anaya asked.

"Yes Mom, I am with you. I have read the mail you had sent me and after reading it, I understood everything. The reason of your leaving the house, the reason for Dad's strange behaviour, and also the truth behind those letters," Olivia said.

"Don't you think that your mother is an extremely selfish woman?" Anaya said wiping her tears.

"Whatever you did, you did for me. You love me so much Mom, you love me the most. Had anyone been in your place, the person would have broken down to pieces and would have quit life. But you smiled with your family, fought with your pain and tried to give me and Dad a life of total happiness and peace. My respect for you has crossed infinity after I came to know what all you had been hiding within your heart all these years," Olivia said holding Anaya's hands.

“A mother’s love made me separate your Dad from his first love, Oli,” Anaya said.

“No one in the world can ever love Dad the way you loved him. Your love for him was totally unconditional, selfless pure. You waited for him for so many years to gain his love, and without any complaints,” Olivia continued.

“For the first time, I am feeling as if I am not talking to my daughter…but rather to a very dear friend of mine,’ Anaya smiled at Olivia.

“I want to be a woman like you, Mom. Just like you, strong, dignified, intelligent and beautiful. You are the most beautiful and loving woman of this universe. If anyone does not realize your worth, it means they do not know to value good things.”

“I have hurt your Dad, Oli. Varsha is now in the last stage of her disease and Nishith can’t see his first love dying in front of his own eyes,” Anaya said with guilt.

“Mom, whatever happened with Varsha masi, it was written in her destiny. Her disease is not because of you. Please don’t blame yourself. You have tried to do the best for her always. Had I been in your place, I would have burnt those letters and never let anything affect my happiness. You gave those letters to Dad; you let him be with his first love. How many women can do that?” Olivia kept saying.

“Your Dad told me that our marriage is over. I am no longer his wife, just the mother of his daughter,” Anaya said regretfully and broke into sobs.

“Yes, that daughter for whom you did everything. Dad does not know the truth Mom. But one day he will, and he will understand you,” Olivia consoled Anaya.

"He won't, Oli."

"He will; he has to. I will make him understand."

"It's not that simple. You have to choose between your parents and I don't want you to undergo this pain. I know you love your Dad the most, so you don't have to think about me. You can live with your Dad if it comes to that extreme of choosing one of us," Anaya said in a trance.

"I am a woman too, Mom, and I can connect with your pain, your struggle and your resilience. I love Dad a lot, but you are like my soul mate Mom. I can never leave you. I am always with you and I have faith in God that He would make Dad realize your worth, your love and your sufferings," Olivia said and hugged her mother again.

"You told me the best thing a mother can ever hear from her daughter," Anaya said with a smile.

"Where is Dad now?"

"He is in New Delhi for Varsha's stem cell therapy. I wanted to accompany him but he refused me. So I came back to my own house, to you."

"You did the right thing. I am with you. Now that you are back, concentrate on your writing again," Olivia said.

"What will be the use?"

"Nothing, I just want you to focus on your career Mom. You are the world's best writer, remember?"

"Love you, Oli. You are truly my soul mate," Anaya said kissing her daughter's cheek.

"Love you too, Mom. Everything will be alright, soon," Olivia said with hope radiating from her eyes as she clutched Anaya's hands.

COPING WITH CHANGE

Everything changes: situation, people, time, place and feelings too. There is no solution in complaining, but rather it is wise to accept the changes occurring around us and within us. After two months of staying with Olivia in Singapore, a call from India gave Anaya the biggest idea of the change that was about to happen in the lives of Anaya, Nishith and Olivia.

"Hello Mom!" Anaya spoke as she received the call of her mother-in-law.

"Anu, Varsha is no more," the news of Varsha's death startled Anaya, freezing all her senses. She knew that Varsha's ailment will ultimately lead her to death someday but she had never expected it to happen so early. Anaya tried to absorb those cruel, bitter words with a palpitating heart and trembling lips.

"Anu, can you hear me?" Anaya's mother-in-law shouted from the other side of the phone to bring back Anaya into her senses.

"When did this happen?" Anaya asked controlling her giddiness.

"Two days back. Nishith is here now, in Kolkata at our place. He is totally lost with Varsha's demise."

"When did Nishith come to Kolkata?"

"Yesterday. He has locked himself in his room and is not talking to anyone else."

"Take care of him, Mom," Anaya managed to say.

"You come here and take care of him. Take him back to Singapore, engage him in work. Do something, Anu. I am scared for him."

"Will he even talk to me now? Doesn't he blame me for whatever has happened with Varsha? It's not a good idea mom. Let Nish stay alone for some time," Anaya said with tears trickling down her face as she thought about the malignant reality that her cousin Varsha had passed away.

"I can't see my son broken down totally; my daughter-in-law and my son have such differences. All these things are too tough for an old woman to digest," Nishith's mother said with a heavy voice.

"I can understand, Mom. Time is too tough for all of us; you take care of Dad and Nish. I will take care of myself and Oli. Bye Mom; I can't talk anymore," Anaya said and disconnected the call with heavy tears choking her breath.

What must have been Nishith's condition on seeing Varsha die in front of his eyes? What would have been uncle and auntie's reaction on hearing of Varsha's death? Why did such a tragedy happen with an innocent girl? She was hardly of my age, and she had to undergo all this. Life is so unfair, but death is simpler than life, I guess. Varsha has died, all her sufferings ended. But what about me? Will Nishith give me a divorce now? Will everything end abruptly between me and him? Will he hate me forever? Will he never forgive me? What will be Olivia's life amidst the tiff of her parents? With whom shall she stay?

All these questions seemed to choke Anaya to death. She dug her fingers inside her pillow, covered her face with the pillow and cried like a baby until Olivia interrupted Anaya's tears by her interrogation.

"Mom, what happened? Look at you. You are sitting on the floor and weeping so badly," Olivia sat on the floor and touched Anaya's shoulders.

"There is a very bad news, Oli. Horrible news from India," Anaya said with heavy breaths.

"Is Dad alright?" Olivia said in a nervous tone.

"Apparently, but he has totally broken from inside due to Varsha's death," Anaya said.

"Varsha masi died? That's so unfortunate," Olivia said, knowing not how to react.

"Somewhere I am also responsible for her fate, Oli," Anaya sobbed.

"Not again Mom. Stop blaming yourself. No one can have any control on someone's death. So please stop blaming yourself again and again. I can understand what you are going through as she is your only cousin sister, but please don't blame yourself for her death," Oli said wiping her mother's tears.

"Your Dad has locked himself up in a room. He is too upset and I can't do anything for him. How unfortunate!" Anaya said shaking her head.

"Shall I talk to Dad?" Olivia suggested.

"No dear. Your Dad needs some time to gain his composure; we should not interrupt his solitude."

"Alright Mom. Let us wait quietly for Dad to be back home."

Anaya nodded her head hopelessly as she knew Nishith would never live in the same house with Anaya again. However, she still hoped against hope that Nishith would return to her soon. Olivia embraced her mother and Anaya felt better.

Ever since Anaya had moved to Singapore again, her daughter had turned out to be her guardian and friend. Her small baby, Olivia had become so matured that she never left her mother alone and always shared every agony and dilemma that Anaya fought. Anaya felt blessed to get such a daughter in this life-time.

That night turned out to be one of the most difficult nights for Anaya. As soon as she closed her eyes, she saw Varsha's face smiling sadly at her, the face which had so many questions imprinted on it. Anaya got up from her bed, made some tea and sat in the balcony of her house at 3 in the morning. Sleep has eluded her as the ghost of Varsha's memories tormented her soul. As she sipped her tea, an old incident with Varsha became vivid to her eyes.

"You know Anu, I just love kids," Varsha had said as she and Anaya went into the nursery of a hospital to see the newborn baby of their neighbour.

"Kids are such a pain, Varshu. They cry your ears off. Kids look good from far, but dealing with them for hours is sheer pain," Anaya had said.

"No silly! Kids are lovely. You know I only want to marry to be a mother. Since I am not a romantic type like you, I don't think I would be having a great love story. However, I want to be a great mother and I want at least two kids, one girl and one boy," Varsha had explained her logic as she looked at the kids sleeping in the nursery.

"That's nice Varshu. I will also give the responsibility of my kid to you. My kid will love her Varsha masi more than her

Mom. So as you will look after my kid, I can go for romantic outings with my future husband," Anaya had teased her excitedly.

"My pleasure... In fact, I feel like adopting a baby right away, but aayi will kill me," Varsha had laughed.

"Yeah, and uncle will faint thinking it is your illegal child. What drama there will be at home!" The two sisters had guffawed loudly.

Anaya's eyes turned moist as nostalgia struck her. She realized that the biggest regret that Varsha had from life must be of not being able to be a mother. Had Varsha been a mother, she would be one of the most loving mothers. Life had been really cruel to her: it did not give her love, did not give her kids, and made her thirst for happiness till she lived. At least, Anaya had Olivia with her in her darkest times, if not Nishith. Anaya felt extremely lucky and went to Olivia's room to find Olivia fast asleep. She thanked God for the most precious treasure of her life and prayed to God for Oli's well-being.

***

It had been two months since the incident and life had been turbulent for all of them.

One fine day, the doorbell rang and Olivia opened the door to find her Dad in front of her eyes. She was seeing him after half a year.

"Dad! Mom, look Dad is here," Olivia screamed with all her vigour and embraced her father.

"How are you, Oli?" Nishith finally spoke to his daughter.

"I was bad as I was missing my Dad terribly. But now I am too happy that you are back, Dad. You don't know how much we missed you."

"I missed you too, dear," Nishith said in a warm voice.

"How are you Nish?" Anaya finally made the initiative to talk to Nishith.

"Better. I want to talk to you. Something very urgent," Nishith said curtly.

Anaya nodded her head and Olivia's face had fear written all over it. She feared that her father would suggest separating. She stood quietly as her parents started talking.

"I am shifting to our old house at Clementi," Nishith said suddenly.

"So you made up your mind for a divorce?" Anaya said looking away.

"I don't know. I need time to think and before I can come to any firm decision, I want to stay in a different place," Nishith said bluntly and Anaya nodded her head in response.

"Please Dad; you can't do this to Mom," Olivia shouted.

"Oli, please go to your room. I will talk to you later," Nishith ordered.

"Listen Dad…I am an adult now and I have the right to speak. I know Mom is innocent and whatever happened to Varsha masi, you can't blame my Mom for it. It was an act of destiny. Mom loves you so much; you can't give her loneliness in return." Olivia tried to explain with a choking throat to her stubborn father.

"Just go to your room, Olivia. Stop interfering in your parents' decisions. Just go!" Nishith said the last two words with such anger that Olivia started crying.

"You scolded me for this! You remember when I used to skip college and school exams, you never scolded me even then, and today you shouted at me for such a small reason. You have changed Dad; you no longer love me or Mom. Only we both love you hopelessly and I hope one day you will realize the depth of our love." Olivia said and left the room with tears.

"You shouldn't have chided her, Nish. It was so insensitive of you," Anaya said.

"Fine! I am insensitive and you are too sensitive," Nishith said sarcastically and packed his belongings and clothes into a bag and left the house, wounding his wife and daughter.

Anaya could not believe that Nishith could change so much. He could hurt his daughter too. Coping with change is a big challenge of our lives, but Anaya wished and prayed that Nishith got back to his original self, no matter how much time it took. Anaya knew she could wait for Nishith forever and would love him with all her heart. It was terrible for Olivia to accept that Anaya and Nishith stayed in different parts of Singapore. She was shattered to see her Mom and Dad, her ideal couple talking only about her if they ever talked over phone. Her Mom and Dad seldom met and she used to stay in her Dad's house on weekends with the motive of making her Dad's mind change, but to no avail. On some nights, Olivia used to cry hugging her mother because of all the change that was ruining their life. Anaya hoped that seeing their daughter's suffering, Nishith would one day change his mind and come back to them. But then again, it was hope against hope.

THE HIDDEN LETTERS

Days went on in the same manner with Anaya and Nishith staying in different houses in the same city. Only Olivia connected them through phone calls sometimes. They never met by plan. Once when they met through coincidence while eating at the same Chinese restaurant, Anaya could see dark circles beneath Nishith's eyes which told her that he was not at peace without her. Had he been happy, he would have glowed and looked healthy. Nishith looked weary. They just exchanged a few customary greetings and started discussing a little about Olivia's studies. As they parted and as Anaya reached her house, she started shaking to the winds of agony hitting her. They had not signed the divorce papers formally, but the current state of affairs between them was similar to divorced couples. Loneliness hugged Anaya not only at the dark hours of night when she went to bed, but also when she woke up from some nightmare with no Nishith to pacify her by her side. She felt lonely when she woke up in the morning, when she made a single cup of coffee for herself, when she read the newspaper, when she cooked, when she watched TV or whatever else she did.

Everything she did, she felt lonely. There seemed to be no cure for her loneliness since months until she locked herself in the study and drowned herself in various books. She read everything, from mythology to books on spirituality to books of travelling. She ditched her bedroom and started sleeping in the study. The study of their house had always belonged to her; she read and wrote there, with her uncountable cups of coffee since she shifted to this place when Olivia was fourteen years old. This place which was masked by the beautiful aroma of books made Anaya forget the tragedies of her own life. The kitchen was adjacent to the study-room and Anaya felt it convenient for her to make as many cups of coffee she needed to drive sleep away from her so that she could read more and more.

Anaya made it her lifestyle: she got up at 8 a.m., made breakfast for Oli and herself, and after Oli left for college, she would again lock herself in the study until her maid would serve her lunch. Some days, she would even skip lunch, until Oli chided her after coming back from college. She would eat some food with Oli, talk to her daughter and then again lock herself with books. Olivia was distressed to find her mother in such a condition. Anaya would hardly meet people, talk to friends, invite anyone home or even write something. Zeeshan called her many times but Anaya never told him a thing.

Olivia made up her mind to do something for her mother and so she brought Zeeshan to their house while returning from college one day.

"Hey, how come you two are together?" Anaya said, startled as she saw Zeeshan and Olivia smiling at her.

"I met Zeeshan on my way and compelled him to make a visit," Olivia said convincingly as Anaya raised her eyebrows at her daughter.

"To the most elegant author on this planet, this one is for you," Zeeshan gave a bouquet of orchids to Anaya.

“There was no need of all this,” Anaya said looking at the flowers.

“Now, will you allow me to step into your house?” Zeeshan said.

“Oh, sure! Come in.”

“How are you Anaya?” Zeeshan asked as Olivia went inside her room.

“Pretty good, rather trying to be,” Anaya said with ease.

“The latter.”

Anaya nodded her head.

“Have you seen yourself in the mirror lately?” Zeeshan asked.

“No, but I can feel that I look like a mess,” Anaya replied.

“You don’t look like a mess. You look like you are doing such a favour to yourself by staying alive,” Zeeshan said as he noticed her eyes, devoid of life.

Anaya nodded her head.

“Have you forgotten your worth, Anaya? You are the best writer of this world, fan mails flood on your website, people wait for your blogs with such enthusiasm and you have made yourself go away from all this. Did you access the internet even once after Nishith left this house? Did you write at least a hundred words? Worse than everything, you told me to not interfere in your matters and here you are, a pale lost woman, drowning yourself within books without caring about your appetite or health or career,” Zeeshan said softly, making each word reach Anaya’s ears clearly.

“What else do I do, Nishith…I mean Zeeshan?” Anaya bit her lower lip realising she had just taken Nishith’s name instead of Zeeshan’s.

"I know you love Nishith intensely, but that does not mean you will subject yourself to such suffering. Don't do this to yourself and to Oli. Do you know how much that kid suffers when she watches you all locked inside the study-room day and night, skipping meals and sleep?"

"I know, but I don't have any idea what I should do, Zee."

"First of all, stop pitying yourself. Look at yourself from a different perspective. You are not a loser. Stop thinking of yourself as a loser; you are a winner. You always have been a winner. How many people can list themselves as the top most writers of this world? How many people can be as self-less as you and face the truth instead of burying it? How many women can be their daughter's inspiration? How many women can be a self-made woman like you? You are the best, Anaya, and it is time you realize your worth once again." Zeeshan explained and Anaya listened comprehending every word he said. She started feeling better somehow.

"I think you are right. I behaved as if my life was over after Nishith left me. I shouldn't have done so," Anaya said.

"Value yourself Anaya; Nishith will also value you again. You have your readers worldwide who love you, admire you and get inspired by you. You have your daughter, you have me as your admirer and you have the Almighty too."

"You are a great friend, Zee. Thanks for restoring the lost confidence in me, once again," Anaya said with a smile.

"I am your biggest fan, after all," Zeeshan smiled too.

"After me, Zee. I am her biggest fan," Olivia said.

"Yeah, sorry. Now listen Anaya, I have a great idea for you," Zeeshan said with a spark.

"I am all ears. Tell me!"

"The world should know your story. The words you wrote for only Nishith and Olivia should be read by all who see you as their inspiration. Make some changes, edit the script by pouring a little bit of fiction and let's give it to the publishers," Zeeshan said.

"Is it a nice story? It does not even have an end," Anaya said after contemplating for a while.

"All stories do not require happy endings. Just edit and end it on a suitable note. People will love it; it is your story. Your readers will feel connected to you."

"Alright, seems like a good idea. I will edit the manuscript, change the names of the characters and let's see if my publishers find it interesting enough to publish it," Anaya laughed.

"Now this is some sort of joke. They will publish without a pinch of doubt and yes, don't change the name of the book. *The Hidden Letters* sounds the best."Anaya nodded her head and Zeeshan wished her luck for her new project. Olivia was happy for her mother and Anaya started editing the script of her own story. Within a month, the publishers approved her story and it was released worldwide within the next six months. It was the seventh novel authored by Anaya and the book created a lot of buzz, since it was inspired from the author's real life incidents. Anaya was a happy woman because of the response her book got worldwide, especially from her Indian readers.

After the huge success of the book, her publishers planned the book launch in three different countries, starting from Singapore. The great event was planned in front of the National Library of Singapore on a Sunday evening. Anaya's in-laws, a few friends and many readers from India came to Singapore for this event. There were journalists from all corners of the world who came to cover the book launch of Mrs. Anaya Chatterjee's seventh novel which was already a huge hit. Anaya was almost exhausted giving interviews over phone before she reached the destination with Olivia and Zeeshan. Anaya saw more than three hundred people sitting in front of her, waiting for her to read out a few excerpts and say something about the book. Anaya had been part of several book launches in the past, but this seemed grand. Anaya took her seat and waved her hands at the people who were assembled there. She smiled at her in-laws and her hopeless heart searched for Nishith in the crowd. Her heart sank when she couldn't find him anywhere.

The event started thereafter with the pretty anchor, Sanjana Arora, giving a small introduction of the book and telling Anaya to unveil the covered book. After the unveiling of the book, which was followed by applauses of people present there, a small AV of Anaya's journey as a writer was shown which included all her six novels which she had written in the past fifteen years. Anaya felt like an extremely proud celebrity whose life story was being shown in the form of an AV. After the AV was shown, it was time for Anaya to say something about her seventh book. And she had been waiting for this moment.

"Thank you everyone for assembling here. My seventh book The Hidden Letters is the story of a woman called Aradhana who had to face her abandoned past as a matter of destiny after many years, which made her enter the quandary of her life. The dilemma whether she should chose happiness or peace, whether she should be true to herself or save her marriage. I hope you all will enjoy reading her life-story and gain motivation to never give up hope in life." Anaya paused for a while when the media started firing questions at her.

"So Mrs. Anaya, is this story influenced from your own life? Is Aradhana actually Anaya?" A journalist asked.

"Yes, this book is inspired from my own life. Aradhana is a mirror image of Anaya," Anaya replied with a smile.

"How does it feel to be an international best-seller of seven books?" Another reporter asked.

"It feels I have known myself better and better with every book I have written. I basically write to know myself and my soul," Anaya answered and there was tremendous roaring of applauses.

"What was the message you wanted to convey through this book?" A reporter asked.

"I wanted to convey that true love reigns over first love. And also that when someone gives up hope, they give up on life too soon," Anaya answered confidently.

"This book has ended on a note where Aradhana is waiting for Naksh with hope in her heart that he will return to her one day, despite Naksh eluding her after the turn of events. Isn't it too much to hope for?" someone else asked.

"Hope is the oil of the lamp called life. If there is no hope in life, there is no life at all. So I have made Aradhana hope against hope without giving up," Anaya replied. "Are you suffering the same plight?" someone from the audience asked.

"Will you elaborate your question please?" Anaya said.

"I mean I have been a great follower of yours. I have attended every book launch of yours and every time, I have seen your husband with you. However, today, he is nowhere to be seen. That made me feel that you are on the exactly same footing as

Aradhana," the woman was about thirty years old. Her asking Anaya such a question made her a little weak in her voice. She was about to answer when she heard a male voice speaking.

"Lady, I feel extremely glad that you have been such a big follower of my wife that you noticed me every time," Anaya recognized Nishith's voice and looked behind to find Nishith smiling at her as he talked over the mike.

"I was in a surgery, so I got delayed. Yes, definitely this book is drawn from incidents of our life but there is a little difference. I was with Anaya, I am with her and I will always be with her." Nishith's words delighted Anaya and she suddenly wanted this event to end so that she could just hug Nishith.

The audience clapped their hands and the biggest applauses came from their daughter, Olivia. The event ended soon after and Nishith pulled Anaya to a corner escaping the eyes of media and the audience.

"I can't believe..." Anaya was about to say when Nishith put his finger on her lips.

"I am sorry Anu. I am sorry that I was out of my mind. Had I read your mail long back, all these misunderstandings would have never occurred. Yesterday when Olivia came to invite me with the card and the book, I started flipping through the pages and read it in a go. I cursed myself so much for being such a brutal beast towards you. I have been staying away from you since all these months but every passing second, I missed you Anu. I have always loved you, but I felt I would be doing injustice to Varsha's soul if

I came back to you. This made me stay away from you. But after reading, I realized that you never did a thing intentionally. You kept hiding those letters from me because of our Oli. You are a great human being, Anu. I have fallen madly in love with you again. Please forgive me."

Anaya took Nishith in her arms as soon as he completed his words.

"I love you Nishith, and I never meant to harm your love," Anaya said gently.

"Varsha was indeed the first woman I fell in love with, but you are my love, my actual true love, my wife and my companion. What we have, it's more than any ordinary love. It's devotion, inspiration and aspiration, too," Nishith said while holding her close to him.

"Our Oli will be so happy to see her parents united again," Anaya said with a peaceful smile.

"Before Oli comes here and finds us, can I take you out for a date?" Nishith asked and Anaya nodded her head happily out of ethereal happiness.

EPILOGUE

Heart of a true woman…
Sublime, arcane and enormous
Veiled with uncountable blood tinted scars
Masked by a layer of unimpeachable strength
Filled with buckets of vigour to love unconditionally
Lined by neat laces of resilience
Weaved with strings of challenges and secrets
Complicated as a newly created spider web
Tangled like a bundle of ropes heaped on
Translucent, not transparent
Trouble-shooter of people relying on it
Soft, not fragile
Determined to cross the limitless ocean of tears
Without giving up singing the song of love
Holding on to memories
Yet strong enough to let go of her loved ones
Not scared of thorns, as she adores her roses
Longing for abundance of love and respect
The heart of a true woman!